"Caramel."

The unexpected reference to candy took her by surprise. "What?"

"Your eyes. They're the color of the caramel my mom used to make for dipping apples when I was a kid. My brothers liked the crunch of hard candy, but I always wanted rich, swirling caramel." His gaze roved over her face, but it wasn't her eyes he finally homed in on.

Kara swallowed hard, biting back the urge to run her tongue over her lower lip. Not in anticipation of a childhood treat, but with a longing for the sweet promise of Sam's kiss. The shock of her own desire was enough to lock her trembling knees in place. "My eyes are brown. Plain and simple."

"Oh, something tells me there's nothing simple about you." His voice held a hint of teasing, but something told her he wasn't joking. That he knew she had her secrets and wouldn't stop until he discovered them all…?

Dear Reader,

Sam Pirelli has been a great secondary character to write. In my first two Clearville books, Sam provided some lighthearted moments as the easygoing, never serious youngest Pirelli brother.

In *Daddy Says, "I Do!"* the challenge was taking fun-loving bachelor Sam and turning him into true hero material. And what better way than to have him discover he's a father?

Kara Starling is Sam's opposite in almost every way. Serious and goal-oriented, she isn't sure Sam is ready to raise her nephew on his own… Maybe because deep down, she's already decided the three of them belong together!

I hope you enjoy Sam and Kara's book!

Happy reading!

Stacy Connelly

DADDY SAYS, "I DO!"

STACY CONNELLY

HARLEQUIN® SPECIAL EDITION®

Recycling programs for this product may not exist in your area.

ISBN-13: 978-0-373-65732-2

DADDY SAYS, "I DO!"

This edition published by arrangement with Harlequin Books S.A.

For questions and comments about the quality of this book, please contact us at CustomerService@Harlequin.com.

Printed in U.S.A.

Books by Stacy Connelly

Harlequin Special Edition

Her Fill-In Fiancé #2128
Temporary Boss...Forever Husband #2148
**Darcy and the Single Dad* #2237
**Daddy Says, "I Do!"* #2250

Silhouette Special Edition

All She Wants for Christmas #1944
Once Upon a Wedding #1992
The Wedding She Always Wanted #2033

*The Pirelli Brothers

Other books by Stacy Connelly available in ebook format.

STACY CONNELLY

has dreamed of publishing books since she was a kid, writing stories about a girl and her horse. Eventually, boys made it onto the page as she discovered a love of romance and the promise of happily ever after.

When she is not lost in the land of make-believe, Stacy lives in Arizona with her two spoiled dogs. She loves to hear from readers and can be contacted at stacyconnelly@cox.net or www.stacyconnelly.com.

To my fellow Special Edition authors—

Reading your books over the years has been a true pleasure. I am thrilled to be one of you and have enjoyed getting to know some of you online and in person. I wish continued success to you all!

Chapter One

Sam Pirelli grinned as he hit the gas on the classic Corvette he'd finished restoring that morning. The body still needed work—dings and dents on the faded red paint showed a lack of appreciation by the vehicle's former owners. But under the hood, she was as good as new.

Better than new, he thought, considering the long hours he'd put in to bring her back to her high-speed glory.

On a straightaway, he could push her to the limit and see how fast she'd really fly, but the winding mountain roads leading back to his hometown were a hell of a lot more fun—the difference between riding on a train and riding on a rollercoaster. Of course, he couldn't go as fast through the twisting turns—he wasn't a total fool—but he knew these roads. And with the way the car was performing, hugging the asphalt and responding to only the slightest tap on the brake or slide of his hand on the wheel, he would swear she knew the way home, too.

The rush of speed and adrenaline fired his blood like little else could. The towering pines along the side of the road whipped by in a blur of dark green and brown, and the clear blue sky held the promise of a gorgeous summer day. With the wind blowing through the open windows, letting in the warm air and the powerful hum of the engine, Sam felt free.

A feeling he cherished more and more, recently.

Almost against his will, he glanced at the wedding invitation on the passenger seat.

Another freaking wedding.

His little sister, Sophia, had gotten hitched a month ago, but under the circumstances, Sam figured a wedding was for the best. Sophia was pregnant and while her new husband, Jake Cameron, wasn't the baby's biological father, everyone in the family knew he was totally committed to being the best husband and father. Jake and Sophia were crazy about each other, and Sam had come to terms with his *baby* sister getting married and becoming a mom.

He could almost hear her protesting that twenty-four wasn't that young. *And neither is twenty-nine, Sam. So when are you going to think about settling down?*

He glanced at the invitation again, already imagining the rented tuxedo's tight fit, and fought the urge to tug at the invisible noose around his neck.

Settling down? Not for him.

He pressed harder on the gas, leaving that thought in the dust.

Of course, less than two months ago, he would have sworn his oldest brother, Nick, felt the same way. He'd been married before and had his heart broken when his wife walked out on him and their daughter. He'd done a hell of a job as a single father for the past five years, and

Sam would have thought he'd be the last guy—okay, second to last guy—to take a walk down the aisle.

But then Nick had met Darcy Dawson, and everything changed. Even Sam could see his brother was more relaxed now, quicker to smile or laugh.

And Sam was happy for his siblings, he really was. He just didn't get it. Didn't understand the need to settle down, to take on the responsibility for someone else's happiness, to give up the freedom of being yourself in exchange for being half of something else....

This time Sam didn't stop himself from rubbing a hand over the back of his neck.

He'd tried talking to his middle brother, Drew, about the crazy rash of weddings striking their family, but when Sam complained about renting a tuxedo *again,* what had his brother said?

Maybe we should think about buying instead of renting.

It was a logical, cost-efficient suggestion, the kind Drew normally made, but something in his brother's distant gaze worried Sam. A look that said Drew wasn't thinking dollars and cents when it came to future weddings but hoping for one of his own.

Sam swore beneath his breath, feeling like the only single guy *not* to drink the commitment Kool-Aid.

Of course his parents were overjoyed. His mother was in a constant state of motion, helping plan one wedding after another with a baby shower for Sophia already in the works. His father was wise enough to stay out of the way, but he hadn't stopped smiling—proud and happy with the additions to the family.

Vince and Vanessa were all about family ties and loyalty and responsibility. Yeah, that word had come up more than once recently.

So had love, a voice whispered through his thoughts. *A lasting love... A love of a lifetime.*

And maybe he had wondered for a lost-his-mind second what it would feel like to have a woman love him the way Sophia loved Jake, the way Darcy loved Nick. But the moment had come and gone faster than the speed limit sign that flew by as he took the next turn.

To have a woman love him that strongly, that completely, well, he'd have to fall for her, too, wouldn't he? And Sam knew he didn't have that depth of emotion inside him. Not anymore. Feelings, like women, came and went.

He liked keeping things fast and fun. He never saw any reason to start digging deeper. He certainly didn't want any woman drilling into him, looking beneath the surface, only to find out what you see is what you get.

Trying to be something he wasn't would only lead down a road to failure, and Sam hated to fail. Hated the raw disappointment of trying his best and knowing it would never be enough.

Shaking off those thoughts, he slowed as he neared town. The sheriff was a good friend's father, but that would only make Cummings come down that much harder. He was glad he had slowed to a reasonable speed as he swerved around some debris in the middle of the road—broken bits of a lumber and trash. A blown-out tire was the next obstacle, and he slowed even more.

Up ahead, he could see a driver who hadn't been as lucky. A light blue minivan was pulled off on the shoulder. It was one of those newer types—the kind meant to fool a family guy into thinking he wasn't really driving a minivan. Only it wasn't a guy who'd been behind the wheel.

A blonde woman stood beside the vehicle, holding up a cell phone as if testing wind speed.

Sam didn't see enough room in the narrow gap between

the road and the tree line to pull up behind her, so he drove past. He half expected the woman to try to flag him down—but the blonde stayed fixated to her useless phone, expecting technology to come to her rescue.

Sam grinned as he parked some yards ahead and climbed from the car. He liked rescuing damsels in distress. Broken-down vehicles were his specialty, of course, but he'd helped more than one ex-girlfriend move and had offered strong and silent support as they gave a current boyfriend the boot. He'd even stepped in a time or two when a whiskey-fueled drunk at the local bar started coming on too strong to a pretty waitress.

He wasn't unfamiliar with a mixed expression of relief and gratitude. But it was not the expression he saw on this woman's face as he drew closer.

Her hair was cut straight to her shoulders in a style that seemed to defy the possibility of a single strand falling out of place. Oversized sunglasses hid her eyes, but beyond the dark frames Sam could see a straight nose, high cheekbones and soft pink lips. Those features were perfect and perfectly free of makeup—this was a woman who thought she had to downplay her looks for the world to see beyond them. Yet it was the stubborn lift to her jaw and the frustration in this woman's stance that caught his attention. She might look calm and cool on the outside, but inside…

He didn't bother hiding a grin as loose gravel crunched beneath his work boots.

The woman was either passing through town or, he hoped, a tourist planning to stay awhile. No way was she local. She was dressed casually enough for travel in dark jeans and a long-sleeved black T-shirt, but even though the soft cotton hinted at curves beneath, the relaxed style didn't seem to fit her the way a pinstriped jacket and pants would have.

Not the type to normally catch his eye. He went for casual, carefree women who matched him one-on-one when it came to having a good time. Except lately, well, he hadn't been enjoying those good times as much as he used to. It wasn't anything he could put his finger on, exactly. More a sense of something missing.

"Need some help?"

Sighing, she dropped her arm but kept her focus on the phone's tiny screen. "I don't suppose your phone would find a signal out here, would it?"

"Nope. But even if it did, it wouldn't do much good since I don't really need it to call myself."

"Excuse me?"

Reaching out, he took the phone from her hand. He powered the tiny thing down and gave it back. Their fingers barely brushed, but the jolt Sam felt in that brief moment should have been enough to fire that phone up for life and send a signal clear to Mars, he thought, unnerved by the instant attraction.

The blonde froze in that same moment, too. A flush rose in her cheeks and her pale lips parted on an unspoken word, a silent awareness that he wasn't alone in the powerful feeling.

Shaking off the crazy thought, he said, "Tow truck, roadside assistance, local mechanic—it's all me."

"All…*you*." This whispered word held a note of recognition as the woman stepped back. The heel of her shoe landed on a rock, and her ankle twisted. She caught her balance before he could reach out to help, her arms held out almost as if warding him off.

Fighting the urge to lift up his own hands in an innocent-man gesture, Sam took a closer look. He swore that behind the dark shades she wore her eyes had widened almost as if she knew who he was. But he didn't see how that was possible.

If they'd met, he would have remembered. Her face, her name, everything about her, especially this pull of attraction. He'd always been the type of guy to appreciate women, to recognize instant chemistry and follow wherever it might lead, and yet this felt different in ways he couldn't explain. "Are you okay?"

"Fine. I'm fine."

Considering she still looked ready to jump out of her skin, Sam reached for his patented grin, thinking to put her at ease, as he held out his hand. "Sam Pirelli, Clearville's local mechanic."

The woman raised her arm automatically, and Sam laughed as he shook her hand around the phone she held. The spark was still there, but he almost breathed a sigh of relief that the wattage was less astronomical this time.

Flustered, she pulled back and slipped the cell into her pocket. "I'm, um, Kara..."

"Well, Kara, this van looks pretty new. I figure you have a spare."

"Yes, of course. I took the van to the dealership for full service before the trip."

Somehow, he wasn't surprised. The woman didn't look the type to leave anything to chance. No detours or what-the-heck side trips for her. He stepped toward the van, but she countered his move almost as if blocking his path. Or trying to, at least, since five-five and a hundred pounds of feminine curves wasn't much of a barricade.

"Look, I know what I'm doing," he reassured her.

The breeze blew a lock of hair into her face, the silken strands catching on her bottom lip, and he rethought his take on her lack of makeup. A light gloss coated her mouth with a hint of color and maybe a touch of flavor. Strawberry, he'd bet. Kara didn't seem the type to go for something like cherry or bubblegum, his young niece's favorites thanks to her fashionable, soon-to-be stepmom, who owned a local cosmetics shop.

Without thinking, he reached up to brush the stray strand back behind her ear. "With cars," he amended, admitting his own reluctance to pull back from the softness of her skin and keep an acceptable, we've-just-met distance. "I've spent the past few months restoring that beauty," he added as he finally took that step back and pointed over his shoulder at the Corvette.

"Months, huh?" A world of doubt filled her voice, and his grin came a lot easier this time.

"I know she doesn't look like much, but it's what inside that counts."

Okay, even he had to admit that sounded like a line, but he didn't think he'd been obvious enough to deserve the sudden suspicion tightening her slender body. It was almost as if she knew what lines he would use and had heard them all before.

Shaking off the odd notion, he gestured to her car. "So, the spare? I can have that flat changed and you can be on your way to…"

"Clearville," she admitted as she stepped back and let him walk over to her vehicle.

"Hey, what do you know? My hometown." Sam decided not to think too closely about the hairpin turn of excitement his pulse took when he realized Kara wasn't simply passing through.

As he walked by the van, a movement in the side window caught his attention. He did a double take when a small face stared back at him from the other side of the glass. A young boy blinked owlishly as if just waking up. He frowned with surprising seriousness, his expression clearing only slightly when he spotted Kara standing outside the vehicle.

She had a kid. Sam supposed he should have expected it, considering the soccer-mom minivan Kara drove, but what he hadn't expected was the sudden jab of disappointment. Kids meant a level of responsibility miles above what he was used to, so he tended to stay away. From kids and from single moms.

"Cute kid," he said, almost automatically, before taking a second glance at the boy in the van.

He was cute. All that blond curly hair sticking up in every direction, the dimple in one sleep-reddened cheek, the wide green eyes beneath straight-set brows. That sense of déjà vu tugged at Sam again. Maybe it was the look in the boy's eyes, he thought. Something a little sad…a little lost, that reminded him of his niece, Maddie, who'd had the same sad, lost look to her eyes when she was that age and still struggling to understand why her mother had left.

Or maybe it was simply the resemblance the boy had to his mother, standing still and silent a few feet away, her arms crossed at her waist. The defensiveness and vulnerability of her stance caught hold of something inside him. An unfamiliar feeling that made him want to shoulder whatever burden she was carrying, break down the carefully constructed walls around her, and let her know everything was going to be okay….

Shoving the crazy thought aside, Sam focused on the one thing he could actually do for the woman and went in search of her spare tire.

Tension had spun her nerves into glass in that brief moment when Sam Pirelli stared at her nephew, and Kara Starling waited for the words that would shatter the last of her composure into a thousand sharp pieces.

Cute kid.

Her breath escaped in a whoosh of sound hidden by the breeze blowing through the pines. Relief left her nearly weak-kneed, and she gave hesitant glance in the mechanic's direction. A soft whistling came from the back of the vehicle as he worked on getting the spare from beneath the van's undercarriage. He didn't seem interested in anything other than changing the tire.

He'd been interested in something more a minute ago, her conscience taunted.

She hadn't missed the spark of attraction that rocked them both when his hand met hers. Sam Pirelli was a gorgeous guy, but then, she'd expected him to be. Dark blond hair peeked out beneath a backward baseball cap that had seen better days. The same could be said for the washed-out gray T-shirt stretched across his wide chest and the threadbare jeans. But Kara was struck by the thought that even a designer suit would fade a little when a woman was caught by the spark in his green eyes and the bright flash of his smile.

Sam Pirelli wasn't the kind of man who tried to impress women. He was impressive without even trying. And his charmer's grin told her he knew it.

And as much as she longed to, Kara couldn't pretend she'd been unaffected by the brush of his warm, rough skin against hers. With anyone else, that magnetic pull of attraction would have been inconvenient. With this man it stirred up feelings of guilt on too many levels to count and whipped already whirling protective instincts into a frenzy.

This wasn't how she'd expected her first meeting with Sam Pirelli to go. But then nothing had gone as Kara expected in the month since her sister had been killed in a plane crash.

Opening the side door to the minivan, she kept her smile

in place when Timmy scrambled back into the booster chair. He dragged his favorite stuffed animal, a slightly cross-eyed green dinosaur, into his lap and hugged it tightly. The boy had always been smart for his age, but also shy and quiet. He'd withdrawn even more since his mother's death, and despite Kara's best attempts she'd been unable to draw him out. Her heart ached for the pain he was feeling and at her own inability to make that pain go away.

"Hey, sleepyhead," she said softly.

After they'd stopped for lunch at a small gas station restaurant along the highway, the little boy had fallen asleep. She'd hoped he would rest for the final leg of their journey, but this unexpected stop had shot that plan out of the water.

Along with her other plan of how to best handle Sam Pirelli.

Awareness of the man working at the back of the van fluttered through her, but Kara pushed it aside and focused on her nephew. When Timmy stayed silent, staring at his shoes over the dinosaur's furry head, she said, "We're almost to Clearville now. Why don't you come on out and walk around for a bit?"

"Then can we go home?" he asked, a heartbreaking amount of hope filling his voice.

Did he think going home would mean returning to the small apartment he'd shared with his mother? That going home would mean finding Marti waiting for him?

Kara took a shallow breath, aware that anything deeper than the slight, tentative motion would cause more pain to her bruised and broken heart. She'd done her best to explain that his mother was in heaven now, where she would always watch over him. But Kara didn't know how much the four-year-old boy understood.

Some days, *she* still didn't understand her sister's death. Not when Marti had been the most alive person Kara had ever known. Her little sister had never done anything half measure. She embraced life and everything in it and rushed into every adventure with a *live for the day* verve Kara had long admired…and envied. But in the end, that never-consider-tomorrow attitude was partly responsible for her sister's death.

Tears burned her eyes, but she blinked them back quickly. Timmy was all that mattered now, and Kara was determined to do right by him and by her sister. Even if it meant taking this trip to Clearville and proving to herself that life in this small northern California town was *not* in Timmy's future.

Though she longed to say they'd be back home in no time, she refused to make promises she might not be able to keep. As much as she loved her sister, Kara knew the young boy had heard his fair share of empty words and promises of tomorrows that had never come.

And now never would.

His mother wasn't going to be there for any of the milestones of his life, or the simple everyday moments so easy to take for granted. The fresh pain of the loss of her sister combined with an old ache Kara refused to acknowledge.

"We're going to stay for a little while," she finally told her nephew.

He heaved a huge sigh. "Okay." And then with the attention span of a typical four-year-old, he scrambled around onto his knees and gazed out the back window. "What's that man doing to our car?"

That man. Sam Pirelli was a total stranger to Timmy. If she kept quiet, he would stay that way. Indecision and guilt tied her stomach into knots. In the month since the reading of Marti's will, Kara had done her best to ignore the feeling, but it was back. *Stronger than ever,* she thought as Sam caught her watching and flashed her a wink.

"His name is Sam Pirelli," she heard herself say softly before she could talk herself out of it. "He's a mechanic, and he's changing out a flat tire for us. Isn't that nice?"

Timmy shrugged, lacking the interest in cars and trucks that most little boys possessed. Reaching out, she smoothed the cowlick stuck up at the top of his head, her fingers sifting through his curls.

Would the hair hidden by Sam Pirelli's baseball cap be as soft?

The wayward thought caught her off guard, and she snatched her hand back as if she'd actually touched Sam's hair. "Why don't we go take a look?"

Timmy climbed from the minivan, clinging tightly to the stuffed dinosaur and to Kara's hand as he looked around. "I don't like it here. It's dark."

"Dark?"

"Uh-huh," he said as he eyed the trees lining the edge of the highway. The thick, dense pines, a far cry from the light, airy palms in San Diego, cast long, jagged shadows and provided a formidable barrier beyond the road. "I think there's monsters."

"Timmy." Kara bit her tongue before she could provide the logical argument that there were no such thing. Monsters might not be real, but the little boy's fears were, and that wasn't something she could "reason" out of him, no matter what her parents thought.

You're only encouraging his fears by pandering to them, her father had argued.

It never failed to amaze Kara how Marcus Starling, a brilliant surgeon, could know everything there was to know about the heart and yet be so clueless about his grandson's feelings.

Honestly, though, she didn't know why she'd been surprised. Her father had never made much of an attempt to understand his daughters either. But his own feelings when it came to this trip had been more than clear.

The fall semester starts in two weeks. You have a responsibility to the college and your students.

Fortunately, her boss at the small private college where Kara taught had been more understanding, lining up part-time teachers to cover her classes in case she needed more time off. Explaining that to her father had been as useless as trying to explain Timmy's fear of monsters.

Have you considered how this leave of absence might affect your chances of being named chair of the department?

Kara already regretted telling her father about the upcoming vacancy. The current chair of the English department was stepping down the next year, and she'd been both surprised and pleased that she was one of the professors under consideration to replace him. But the position was anything but a sure thing and if the faculty chose another teacher...well, it wouldn't be the first time she'd disappointed her father.

Giving a resigned sigh, Kara gave her nephew's hand a reassuring squeeze. *We all have our monsters, don't we, Timmy?*

Before she could come up with a response to soothe her nephew's fears, the off-key whistling from the back of the van was followed by a soft thud. Kara turned to watch Sam Pirelli lift the spare. The faded cotton stretched across his wide shoulders, and the bulge of his muscular thighs tested the worn seams of his jeans as he crouched down to maneuver the tire into place.

Kara swallowed, her mouth drier than the mild temperature could account for.

"Wow, he's superstrong."

The whistling stopped for a moment at Timmy's awe-filled comment, only to start up again a little louder, and if possible, a little cockier. The flush of embarrassment on her face burned hotter when Sam glanced over his shoulder with a knowing grin. It was almost as if he'd overheard *her* raving about his super strength, which was ridiculous because she certainly wasn't impressed with his muscular arms or chest or—

Oh, who was she kidding? She was just as impressed as her nephew, if for very different reasons. She could only hope she was slightly better at hiding it.

"Okay, you're good to go. You'll want to replace the spare before you head home…" His voice trailed off as if expecting her to fill in where she was from, but that, like her last name, was information Kara wasn't willing to give.

"I'll do that."

"Here." Reaching into his back pocket, he pulled out a business card and handed it to her. "Stop by the shop and I'll set you up."

"Thank you. What do I owe you?"

He shook his head before she could finish the question. "Don't worry about it."

Kara frowned. She didn't like being indebted to anyone, and she was especially uneasy about owing Sam Pirelli. Maybe because, deep down, she knew what she owed him most of all was the truth. Shoving the thought aside, she said, "I owe you for your time."

"Okay, then." The glint in his eyes should have warned her what was coming, but she was still caught off guard when he announced, "Dinner."

"Excuse me?"

"You said you wanted to repay me, so I'm thinking dinner. Nothing too fancy. It was just a tire, not like replacing the carburetor or anything."

His smile threatened to shake something loose inside her. What would it be like to have those teasing lips flirting with hers? Her heart skipped a beat, but she'd long ago learned the dangers of dancing to that foolish rhythm. "I don't think that's a good idea."

"Hey, it was your idea in the first place. You're the one who insisted on paying."

"And you always take sandwiches over cold hard cash?"

"I was thinking maybe steak and potatoes, but if you're craving sandwiches—"

Throwing her hands out to her sides, Kara protested, "I did not say I was craving sandwiches!"

Sam grinned again, stopping any further protest as she realized he wasn't looking at her. Glancing down, she saw Timmy watching the exchange with wide-eyed interest. He looked slightly puzzled, as if wondering what his normally calm, cool and collected aunt was doing standing on the side of the road, arguing with the most infuriating man.

It was a question she had to ask herself, and she felt her face heat as she looked back at Sam. Seeming to realize he'd pushed as far as he should, he flicked the edge of the business card she still held. "Don't forget to get that tire replaced."

He turned to walk back to his beat-up-looking car, and Kara knew she should let it go. Just let him walk away. But the words escaped before she could stop them and she called out, "I'm going to pay for the new tire."

He turned with his hand braced on the driver's side door. "No problem. I'm all for dessert, too. You know where to find me when you decide what you're hungry for."

The ridiculous, arrogant parting line was still ringing in her ears when Sam's car sped off with a squeal of tires and cloud of dust. *What she was hungry for...*

Kara snorted in response as she helped Timmy back into his booster seat. When it came to men like Sam Pirelli, she was on a permanent diet!

"What'd you say, Aunt Kara?"

"Nothing, sweetie." Looking up from snapping the belt at his waist, her heart stuttered as she met the little boy's gaze. She swallowed as recognition hit hard, and an unwanted thought drifted through her mind for the first time.

He has his daddy's eyes.

Chapter Two

As Sam walked into his garage later that morning, he spotted a familiar pair of worn work boots and skinny, jeans-clad legs sticking out from beneath a navy sedan. Even though Will Gentry had been working for him since the beginning of summer, Sam still wasn't one hundred percent accustomed to someone else in his shop.

He had long prided himself on taking care of his customer's cars as if they were his own—doing all the maintenance and repairs, and not letting anyone else lend a hand. Thanks to that work ethic, he was busier than he could handle, to the point of turning work away. Hiring an employee had been a big step, but it was only the beginning of plans that included the Corvette he'd parked out front.

A grin tugged at his lips when he thought about Kara's obvious lack of appreciation for the work he'd done on the car. Obviously she wasn't easily impressed. What would it take, he wondered, to really wow a woman like her?

Anticipation fueled the blood in his veins even though he wasn't sure what to make of his undeniable interest. He didn't usually go for serious types. Or single mothers, he reminded himself. Knowing Kara had a son should have been enough to keep his mind off the woman, beautiful or not. But she was only visiting. So, it wasn't as if he was expecting anything permanent. Just a chance to get to know the lady, short-term, until she was ready to move on.

"How's it going, Will?" Sam asked, turning his attention back to his young assistant. One good thing about having an employee was having someone to talk to. With Will, that meant having someone who listened, but rarely responded beyond a mumbled word or two.

The grunted response from under the sedan was less verbose than usual, but Sam knew the simple oil change wasn't enough to give Will any trouble. "Come on out for a minute, will ya?"

Moving in slow motion, Will's scuffed heels inched along the concrete, revealing more of his threadbare jeans, then a ratty yellow T-shirt over a nearly skin-and-bones torso, until finally Sam got a glimpse of the kid's face—and the black eye he'd been reluctant to reveal.

Sam frowned as the kid tucked his legs up beneath him. "What happened, Will?" he demanded even though the fist-shaped bruising around the boy's swollen eye told the story. "Or should I say who?"

Smart, skinny and shy, Will could easily be the target of bullies, and Sam felt a protective instinct to step in and defend the kid. By the time he was Will's age, he'd filled out enough that his size alone silenced the insults that had done more damage than any physical fight.

"It was my fault," Will mumbled, refusing to meet his gaze. "I started it."

"Oh, really," Sam said, deadpan. Will was a good kid. Not the kind to get into trouble or cause fights.

"Look, if some kid's been bullying you, you can tell me."

Will kept his head down, as if Sam might forget about the black eye if he didn't look him in the face. "It's not some kid. It's— Something I can handle."

"If you want, I can show you some ways to defend yourself."

"Yeah, right." Will paused. "The guy's like twice my size."

"Self-defense isn't about being bigger than your opponent, you know."

Will snorted as he stood and glanced between Sam's six-foot-three-inch, two-hundred-pound frame and his own five-seven and buck-twenty-five. "Easy for you to say."

"Hey, I wasn't always this size, and growing up I had two older brothers who used to gang up on me. It felt like they'd always be bigger and stronger and that no matter how much I grew, I'd never catch up."

Sometimes it still felt that way. As if his brothers' successes and accomplishments were somehow greater than his own.

It wasn't that he was jealous of his brothers. He was proud of them. And, okay, so Nick and Drew had gone to college—Nick to be a veterinarian and Drew to study architecture before he decided he preferred building to designing—while Sam had struggled far more than he'd let on to just finish high school.

His brothers had been the good students, and he'd been the troublemaker, the class clown. All his life he'd heard the same comments from his teachers, his parents, even his high school girlfriend. *If you'd just try harder...*

The hell of it was, he *had* tried. He could remember being ten or eleven years old and sweating bullets as he struggled to finish a test or a project or a reading assignment. But he'd been unable to focus, to concentrate. His mind would drift away. Soon his gaze would follow and before long he'd have to escape. To be outside where he could run and play and forget.

By the time he hit junior high, he realized failing without trying was easier. He doubted he could explain it, but to his frustrated, angry mind, it had made sense. If he didn't study, if he didn't do his homework, if he didn't complete assignments, he had a built-in excuse for failing. All it meant was that he was lazy, a goof-off who lacked discipline. If he tried and failed, well, that meant he was stupid, didn't it?

When he reached high school, he discovered an alphabet's worth of acronyms for learning disabilities. Part of him had been relieved to discover a reason for his problems, but by then keeping those difficulties a secret for the sake of his social standing had been second nature.

So he'd continued to hide his weakness behind an easy laugh and a what-the-hell smile and managed to get through high school. Barely. God, he'd been so scared, nearly sick to his stomach, his entire senior year. Terrified that he'd fail a class so badly his teachers would hold him back when all he wanted was to get out. Stuck behind a desk, crowded inside four walls, he'd itched for freedom, desperate to escape and unable to sit still.

Even though the worst of his symptoms had faded as he grew older, something his online research had told him didn't always happen, that same feeling still snuck up on him when he thought about settling down. Trapped by a white picket fence instead of the chain link that circled the high school, but trapped all the same.

Shaking off those memories, Sam told Will, "If you

change your mind and decide you'd like some help, let me know."

"Just forget it, okay, Sam? I can take care of myself."

Sam recognized the defiant lift to the boy's chin and knew he wasn't going to get any more out of Will. But patience had never been Sam's strong suit. He wanted to push, to keep driving and get to the bottom of what Will had said—and whatever it was he was trying not to say.

Deciding to leave the ball in Will's court for now, he nodded toward the sedan. "Think you can take care of this oil change?"

Will nodded, relief filling his young features.

"All right, then. Get back to work."

Following his own advice, Sam checked the inventory for a replacement tire for Kara's minivan. Even though she hadn't told him where she'd be staying, he could easily find out. But for now it was another opportunity to play it cool. He'd given her the perfect excuse to see him again. If she didn't take it—well, then he'd have to come up with an excuse of his own.

Never, in her wildest imagination, had Kara dreamed of being a spy. She'd never tried opening a lock with an unfolded paperclip. Never sent away box tops from sugary cereal for a secret decoder ring. Never tried eavesdropping with a glass pressed against a door.

Just as well, she decided, as she sank further down behind the steering wheel. Because she certainly would have been very, very bad at it. Not that she was actually spying. She'd parked beneath a shady spot across the street from Sam Pirelli's garage fifteen minutes ago, the windows rolled down to catch a breeze carrying the scent of surrounding pines, but she wasn't spying.

You aren't going to find out anything about the man unless you really get to know him.

The voice of Olivia Richards, her best friend, rang in her thoughts. Olivia was a fellow teacher and the only person besides Kara's parents to know the reason she had made the trip to Clearville.

Unlike her parents, Olivia had supported Kara's decision to find Sam Pirelli.

"I can't believe you met him already. What are the odds?" her exuberant friend had demanded when Kara phoned her after checking in at a local hotel and settling Timmy down for a nap. "It's like fate."

"It is not fate."

Olivia snorted. "You break down in the middle of nowhere and the very guy you've traveled hundreds of miles to see is there to change your tire. That *is* fate, Kara-girl."

"He's a mechanic. He was doing his job, not riding in to save the day on his trusty steed, okay?" Kara wasn't sure who she was trying to convince. Sam Pirelli's arrival had very much smacked of a white-knight rescue whether she wanted to admit it or not.

Her friend sighed. "Fine, so he was simply in the right place at the right time. Tell me what he's like."

"He's—he's like too many of Marti's past boyfriends," Kara said dismissively. "Good-looking and out for a good time."

"How good-looking?" Olivia pressed, curiosity clear in her voice even from miles away.

"Are you even listening to me?" Kara had demanded in a whisper as she glanced to the bedroom door only a few feet away from the suite's tiny living area.

"I heard you say he was good-looking. In all the years we've known each other, you've been blind to the opposite sex."

"Not blind," Kara murmured, her friend's teasing words stinging a little even though she knew they shouldn't. The truth was, she'd been blinded by love before, and she'd sworn she'd never be so vulnerable again. "And you missed the part where I said Sam Pirelli's only out for a good time."

And not father material.

Kara might not have said that last part out loud, but Olivia had been her friend long enough to hear the unspoken accusation. "How do you know after one meeting?"

"I just know," she argued. When her friend's silence continued, she blurted out, "He hit on me, okay? Five minutes into meeting the guy, and he was pushing for a dinner invitation. What does that tell you?"

"Um, that's he's interested in you?"

"He's a player, Liv. He'd hit on anything with a pulse."

"You don't know that."

But Kara felt she did. Knew the type, at least. The kind to make promises, to vow to love a girl forever. But she'd learned those words—like those men—were meaningless.

"You have to give him a chance," Olivia encouraged. "Weren't you the one who said it was wrong of Marti to keep Timmy's birth a secret?"

"I know, but Marti must have had her reasons, right?"

And what those reasons were…the possibilities made Kara sick to her stomach when she thought of handing Timmy over to the stranger who was his father. As much as she'd loved her sister, she'd never understood Marti's attraction to rough and rowdy men.

But Sam's not like that.

The voice that sounded so much like Marti's whispered through Kara's mind. On the surface, at least, Sam was more the golden-boy-next-door type than dark and dangerous. He had a quick and easy smile, a good sense of humor and a willingness to laugh at himself.

All…not bad qualities.

Kara could see why Marti would have found him attractive. But her sister had excelled in picking men suited for short-term relationships. None of them had been built for the long haul. Even if he didn't possess the worst qualities of some of Marti's previous boyfriends, was Sam Pirelli the type of man to put the needs of a child before his own?

"You may never know what made Marti keep silent in the past. But I think in that letter she was pretty clear about what she wanted for the future."

The letter. The one that had sent Kara on this mission in the first place.

The shock of her sister's death in a small plane crash had been like a nightmare. Too horrible and unreal to be true. Kara had sleepwalked through those first days, waiting for someone to wake her up. But reality had set in quickly, forcing grief aside. After all, she had Timmy to think about.

Finding out her carefree sister had a will had come as another shock. And the letter naming Timmy's father for the first time and asking Kara to take the little boy to meet Sam Pirelli had been the last painful blow.

How could you ask me to do this, Marti? How could you ask me to give up a child I love as if he were my own?

But if Marti's voice had spoken before, it was silent now, leaving Kara's raw and aching questions unanswered.

After the reading of the will, Kara had talked with the lawyer. Because Marti had named Kara her son's legal guardian, he reassured her, in the eyes of the law, Timmy was hers…as long as the boy's father didn't sue for custody. Then, the lawyer told her, the courts tended to side on behalf of the biological parent.

She swallowed hard, the sign for Sam's Garage blurring before her eyes as she blinked away the hot press of tears.

She didn't know for sure that her sister wanted Sam to

raise their son. Didn't even know if Sam Pirelli would want to take on that responsibility.

Inhaling a deep breath, she forced the rush of emotion aside. She had two weeks to find out. That was the time-frame she'd given herself, one that coincided with the start of the fall semester and also the beginning of the year at the preschool where Timmy was enrolled.

"Aunt Kara." She glanced in the rearview mirror to meet her nephew's disgruntled gaze. "I wanna go home."

That refrain, coupled with "are we there yet?" had repeated with headache-inducing consistency over the past two days. "I know, sweetie." Turning around in the seat to face her nephew, she said, "Do you remember the man who changed our tire? Well, we need to go to his garage and replace the one that went flat."

"But why are we just sitting here?" He drummed his heels against the edge of the seat, revealing his impatience.

"Because Mr. Pirelli is…busy."

And he had been since the moment Kara parked the van across the shop. The prosaically named Sam's Garage looked like the kind of place that would have a girly calendar pinned to a wall, but it was Sam who could hold his own with Mr. November any day.

Even from across the street, she could see the wink of his dimples, the flash of bright white teeth, the crinkles at the corners of his eyes. Little wonder women fell for him, and from what she had witnessed, Sam Pirelli did not discriminate.

A tall, stunning redhead had stopped by, followed by a short, curvy blonde. He greeted them with that killer smile and exchanges were made—keys, cars, laughter, embraces. A petite, doe-eyed brunette then brought him a late lunch in a brown paper bag—a huge sandwich he ate with the gusto of a man who was starving. Not that Kara believed it.

With so many women flocking around, going without hardly seemed necessary. Or even possible.

All of which made her wonder again what her sister had been thinking.

It also made Olivia's advice ring through her thoughts again.

And once the brunette left, Kara decided this might be her best opportunity to get to know Timmy's father. "All right, Timmy. It looks like Mr. Pirelli has some free time now."

And as long as no other women stop by, maybe he can squeeze in a few minutes for the son he's never known.

The thought was more than a little unreasonable, but then again, so was the jealousy she'd felt. She'd told Olivia the man was a playboy, flirting with any woman who crossed his path. That his interest in her and his angling for a dinner date meant nothing. But watching proof of her words brought to light right in front of her made her feel foolish for thinking she might have been wrong.

The motor roared in protest as she turned the key, forgetting she already had the engine running. Even more flustered now, she sucked in a calming breath as she pulled out of her hiding place and drove the minivan the short distance into the garage's parking lot.

She'd barely set one foot on the ground before Sam appeared, opening the door the rest of the way and offering her a hand.

"Come for that spare?" he asked with enough question in his voice to suggest she might have shown up for another reason. Like the dinner he thought she owed him.

"That's why I'm here. For the tire." One that, hopefully, wasn't as overinflated as Sam's ego.

Even though they'd only met that morning, Kara had already tried to convince herself he wasn't that tall, his shoulders weren't that wide, his smile wasn't that tempting. That in an effort to distract her emotions, her mind had simply exaggerated, focusing on unimportant details and blowing them all out of proportion. That was what she'd told herself. Unfortunately, Kara realized as she gazed up into his handsome face, she'd lied.

He didn't give any ground as she stood, keeping her caught between the V of the open door and his body. His eyes searched hers as if looking for answers to questions he'd yet to ask, and Kara's heartbeat stumbled uncertainly. Standing this close, she could smell the unfamiliar combination of motor oil and machinery, but also the clean, simple, sexy scent of the man beneath.

"Caramel."

The unexpected reference to candy took her by surprise. "What?"

"Your eyes. They're the color of the caramel my mom used to make for dipping apples when I was a kid. My brothers liked the crunch of hard candy, but I always wanted rich, swirling caramel." His gaze roved over her face, but it wasn't her eyes he finally honed in on.

Kara swallowed hard, biting back the urge to run her tongue over lower lip. Not in anticipation of a childhood treat, but with a longing for the sweet promise of Sam's kiss. The shock of her own desire was enough to lock her trembling knees in place. "My eyes are brown. Plain and simple."

"Oh, I'd be willing to bet there's nothing simple about you." His voice held a hint of teasing, but something told her he wasn't joking. That he knew she had her secrets and wouldn't stop until he discovered them all. "You had sunglasses on earlier. For some reason with your blond hair and fair skin, I expected your eyes to be blue."

Another shock quaked down her spine, and Kara braced

a hand against the side of the minivan. Sam stepped back, giving her room to breathe, but she still felt lightheaded after his casual revelation.

Marti's eyes had been blue.

While Kara had worried about Sam's paternal instincts coming to the fore and that he might somehow recognize Timmy as his son, she'd given little thought to him realizing she was Marti's sister. Though the two of them had the same coloring and bone structure, the similarities ended there. Her sister had been taller, blonder, hiding her fair skin behind bronzers and spray-on tans.

"Aunt Kaaaraaaa!" Timmy's impatient call from the backseat broke through her panic, and she ducked past Sam to open the door.

"Sorry, Timmy. Come on out, okay?"

The boy nodded, but his attention was clearly on the man standing behind her, a mix of curiosity and interest in his green eyes.

Sam's eyes.

And Kara knew in that moment, everything had changed. Whether or not she told Sam about the boy he'd unknowingly fathered, she would never be able to look at her nephew the same way again. The weight of the secret she kept made her long to jump back in the van and drive as far as she could to escape the responsibility.

If the seriousness of the choice she had to make hadn't been so great, Kara might have laughed. Running from responsibility. That was something she'd never done as an adult. Reaching up, she touched the locket she wore around her neck. For the past twelve years, she'd lived her life on the straight and narrow, determined to make the right choices. To do the right thing.

But what was the right thing? To tell the truth? Or to keep her sister's secret?

Realizing she wasn't going to come to a decision right then, Kara held out her hand as Timmy climbed from the backseat, his dinosaur tucked beneath one arm.

"Aunt Kara?" Sam echoed, a hint of surprise lifting his eyebrows, and Kara realized he must have assumed Timmy was her son.

"Um, yes. It's—it's a long story." One she wasn't yet prepared to tell. "About that tire—"

"Right." He nodded once, seeming to accept her desire to get down to business. "Will can change it out for you while we handle the paperwork," he added as they walked toward the garage.

For the first time, Kara noticed a skinny young man bent over an open hood. As Sam spoke his name, the teen looked up with a nod. A dark bruise blacked one eye, and he ducked his head after only a split second of contact.

"I have some toys in the office." Sam held open the door to a small office that seemed to have been tacked on to the side of the garage like an afterthought. "Bunch of cars and trucks my mom saved from when I was a kid. And then my sister Sophia added some dolls and stuff in case a little girl wanted to play."

"Girls can't play with cars and trucks?"

Sam raised a hand as if she'd proved his point. "That's what I said, but she seemed to think they'd like Barbie better."

The office was small and crowded with a desk, file cabinets and mismatched chairs, but it was the narrowness of the doorway Kara noticed most as her shoulder brushed Sam's chest as she passed.

"There's the toy box right over there, Timmy," Sam said, gesturing to a box with a monogrammed yellow *S* on the front nearly faded away.

The boy hesitated, scraping his tennis shoe along the

scuffed linoleum floor, and Kara said, "He's not really into cars and trucks."

Sam nodded knowingly. "All about the electronics for kids these days, isn't it? Video games and computers."

"I suppose, but Timmy likes books and puzzles." She could sense Sam's surprise in the look he shot at the boy. Feeling more and more defensive by the minute, she insisted, "He's very smart for his age. He's been going to a very prestigious preschool since he turned three. School's starting again in another two weeks, and he's looking forward to getting back and seeing his teachers and his friends."

"Whatever he likes to do, right?"

Kara swallowed and strove for a sense of calm that had completely deserted her. Her heart was racing and she felt out of breath, all without reason. Sam hadn't challenged a single thing she said, but even though he didn't know it, he was a roadblock in front of all the plans she had for her nephew. "Right. It's all about what's best for Timmy."

If she could only determine what that was....

"Hey, good choice, my man." Sam grinned over her shoulder and Kara looked back to see her nephew holding a tiny red metal car in his hand. A car that even she could see looked very much like the one Sam drove.

"Now that is a familiar sight," he added.

Kara swallowed against the rising panic. Was it only that car Sam recognized, or on some level was he starting to see a younger version of himself in the green-eyed, blond-haired boy?

Her heart tumbled inside her chest as Sam crouched down, folding his big body until he could meet Timmy's gaze face-to-face. When he held out his palm, the boy's face fell and he reluctantly handed over the car. "No, Timmy. You can keep the car. I wanted you to give me five."

He shot a confused look at Kara. "Five what?"

"Give me five. That's what it's called when I hold out my hand and you slap my palm with yours."

Eyes wide, Timmy shook his head. "I'm not supposed to hit."

"It's not hitting. It's..." Sam glanced over his broad shoulder as if looking for some help in this department, but Kara could only shrug.

Clearly both she and Marti had been lax when it came to explaining the high five. The gesture wasn't exactly one that filled her daily life, though she realized it was a guy thing. High fives. Chest bumps. Those complicated handshakes. They were all signs of male celebration and camaraderie that were completely beyond Kara.

Was that why Marti had asked Kara to find Timmy's father? To provide the boy the male role model missing from the first four years of his life?

"You know what? Don't worry about giving me five." Lowering his voice, he added, "But I want to tell you something about that car. A car like that is super-fast."

His eyes wide as if understanding Sam was imparting some kind of secret knowledge, her nephew whispered, "How fast?"

"Faster than a bird or a bear or..." Sam's voice trailed off but not before a look passed between man and boy.

An unspoken communication that shook Kara to the core even as Timmy filled in, "Monsters?"

Sam bumped his fist against the one Timmy had closed around the small car. "You better hold on to that. Just in case."

A sudden clatter of metal against concrete broke the moment. Sam's head swung back toward the open doorway to the garage and pushed to his full height with a frown when a muffled curse followed. "Will," he called, "you break anything important out there?"

At first only a pained silence answered before the teen responded, "Just my foot."

"In that case, get back to work."

Kara gaped at the callous response and took a step toward the door. "Don't you think—"

Reaching out, Sam wrapped a hand around her arm, stopping her progress, her words, her heartbeat. For a crazy moment, she imagined him pulling her closer, his eyes darkening as he kissed her.

"He'll be fine."

It took a moment for Kara's mind to refocus on Sam's words instead of his touch. "You don't know that."

"I know if we rush out there and start hovering over Will, it will only make that bruised foot feel worse."

"That doesn't even make sense."

He gave a short laugh at that. "Because it's guy logic. You'll have to trust me on this one. If we pay any attention to him right now, it'll hurt his pride and embarrass the he…heck out of him. For a kid like Will, that's worse than broken bones any day."

As if proving the truth—logical or not—of his words, the high-pitched whine of machinery resumed as Will went back to work.

"Will's shy and quiet, but he's tough in his own way."

A hint of pride and admiration filled Sam's voice. Admiration for the teen's toughness? Kara wondered.

A toughness that Timmy, with his reluctance to hit and his fear of monsters, didn't possess.

"He's just a boy," she protested, not sure if she was talking about Will or Timmy. "Do you really think ignoring pain is the best way to deal with it?"

Half expecting some quick response about rubbing dirt

on a wound and getting back in the game, Kara was surprised when Sam gave her question some thought. "Admitting you're hurting makes you vulnerable. Hiding that pain's a pretty good way to make sure no one can make that hurt even worse."

Memories of her own hidden pain pushed to the surface, but Kara forced the thoughts aside even as she wondered if she and Sam might have something in common. "I wasn't exactly suggesting that you go out there and slam Will's hand in a car door to make him forget about his foot."

Sam laughed and the moment was broken, the quick grin on his handsome face almost enough to wipe away the thought of this big, strong man being vulnerable to anything—or anyone. "As far as distractions go, I can think of a few that would be more enjoyable."

Kara barely had time for a blush to rise to her cheeks before he turned his focus to business. "Now, if I can take a look at your driver's license, I can use that into to get you into the computer." Jiggling the mouse on his desk, a screen popped up marked with blanks.

Information Sam was waiting to fill in. Information like her last name and where she was from. Pieces of a puzzle that might become a clear picture if she told him anything more about herself. She glanced over at the toy box where Timmy was carefully guiding his car along the well-worn edge. On some level, Sam had already picked up on her resemblance, faint though it was, to Marti. Add in the last name they shared and the city where they'd both lived, and he was bound to put the pieces together.

"Kara?"

Sam gazed at her from across his desk, waiting for her to hand over her license. Nerves shook her stomach as she realized she'd been wrong. She'd thought telling Sam he was Timmy's father might be the biggest mistake she could make. But having him figure it out *before* she told him would be so much worse.

Without letting herself stop to think, she said, "What about that dinner I owe you?"

Her forced smile started to tremble along the edges as Sam's slightly surprised gaze met hers. Did he see right through to her ulterior motives? Or could she fool him into thinking her nerves were due to accepting his date?

His green eyes lit with pleasure, and Kara's stomach pitched in a slow, shaky roll. *Were* her nerves more about going out with Sam than she wanted to admit? She'd have to worry about that later. For now, she breathed a sigh of relief when Sam moved his hand away from the mouse.

"Tonight?"

"Um…" His eager question caught Kara off-guard. If she didn't know better, she might think this "date" really mattered to Sam. But she did know better, didn't she?

He's interested in you.

"Sorry," he said, his smile turning a little embarrassed and slipping further past her defenses. "I forgot you just got into town. You probably want to take it easy and get Timmy settled. How about tomorrow?"

"Tomorrow?"

"Hey, I eat dinner every day, so take your pick."

Kara couldn't help giving a startled laugh at Sam's dogged pursuit. With his good looks and quick smile, she'd assumed a man like Sam Pirelli treated everything in life as easy come, easy go. But in the past few minutes, he'd shown a depth and determination she hadn't expected.

"And I can ask Hope Daniels to babysit Timmy," he added. "She's a friend of the family who watches my niece, so you don't have to worry about her. She's very reliable."

But as they finalized plans for their date the following

night, Kara was already worried. She just couldn't decide what concerned her more—the idea of Sam's single-minded focus on Timmy…or on her.

Chapter Three

"Hey, Sam!"

Pausing outside Rolly's Diner after closing up his shop for the evening, Sam turned to see Billy Cummings climb from his truck. An old friend from grade school, the two of them had shared a friendship and rivalry for the past two decades.

"Someone said they saw a piece-of-crap 'Vette limping down the highway this morning. You didn't get that pile of junk running, did you?" Challenge rose in the other man's expression, and Sam knew the sheriff's son was ready for anything—a hearty slap on the back or a sharp jab to his jaw.

Sam went with his first instinct and chuckled even though he hadn't completely forgiven the other man. "If you knew a thing or two about cars, you would have realized what a prize that 'piece of crap' really is."

The car's original owner had first contacted Billy, knowing how Cummings liked fast cars, but Billy didn't have the skills needed to get the Corvette back in prime condition and he knew it. When he passed on making an offer, the owner had called Sam. He'd jumped at the chance to buy the classic only to end up in a bidding war with Billy, who might not have wanted the car but didn't want Sam to have it either. In the end, Sam bought the 'Vette, but thanks to Billy, at a much higher price.

"Have you decided what color to paint it?"

"I'm sticking with red."

Billy shook his head. "You might as well paint it black now, since you're gonna end up selling it to me."

"Yeah, right." Sam scoffed. He had bigger plans for the car than handing it over to his friend. The year and model were rare enough that he had a good idea what the restored car would draw at an auction. He wasn't new to auctions or the kind of crowd and car enthusiasts they attracted. As much as he liked working at the garage, restoring classic cars was his true passion and his dream for the future.

Clearville was home, and he had no plans to leave, but the thought of traveling around to car shows throughout the state, buying "pieces of crap," restoring them and then selling them for a small fortune...yeah, he liked that idea a lot.

"You missed your chance to own that car, my friend," he told Billy. "You'll be lucky if I even let you ride in it."

Climbing back into the cab of his truck, Billy vowed, "Just wait."

"For what? A cold day in hell?" Sam laughed as his friend pulled away with an obnoxious honk of his horn. He was still smiling as he pulled the door to the diner open and walked into the familiar scents of fried food and strong coffee.

A waitress greeted him and asked, "Your usual table, Sam?"

The back corner table at Rolly's might not have had the

Pirelli brothers' names on it, but all the staff and locals knew it was theirs. The "newer" section of the restaurant, added on some twenty years ago, was filled with large-sized tables. And the Pirelli brothers were large-sized men. Guys who didn't do booths.

It was one thing to be on a date, sitting close to a pretty girl, thigh touching thigh, holding hands beneath the privacy of the table. He had no trouble with the idea of sharing a booth with Kara.

But a couple of broad-shouldered guys crammed together like that? No way.

He started to nod to the waitress when a familiar face caught his eye. Nadine Gentry, Will's mother, had worked at Rolly's for almost as long as Sam could remember. "I'll take one of the booths tonight, thanks."

Will hadn't said anything more about the fight, but Sam sensed something was on the kid's mind. Sam had few rules, but keeping your mind on the job was one of them. Not paying attention was a surefire way to end up hurt.

Sam had promised he'd let Will handle his own problems, but that didn't mean he couldn't ask Nadine if she was worried about her son.

An older, feminine version of Will, Nadine's black T-shirt and denim skirt hung from her slender frame, the dark color stark against her pallid complexion and fair hair. "Hey, Sam, what can I get you?" she asked, pulling out a small notepad from her red apron and fiddling with her pen instead of meeting his gaze.

Pretending to hesitate over the menu, he said, "I need just a minute. How are things going?"

She shrugged a narrow shoulder. "Busy. Tips have been good."

"And Will?" Was it just his imagination or had the woman tensed at the mention of her son's name?

"You'd know that better than I would, Sam. He's at your place more than he's at home."

With school still out for another few weeks, Will had been spending a lot of time working. For the first time, though, Sam wondered if it wasn't something other than a need for extra cash that had the teen spending so much time at the garage. "He didn't get that black eye at my shop."

Nadine paled slightly, but she defiantly held his gaze. "What are you saying, Sam?"

Sam didn't pay much attention to Clearville gossip, but he had heard that Nadine had hooked up with a younger man. Sam had never liked Darrell Nelson, a grudge that went back to their days on the playground, when Darrell had taken pleasure in picking on anyone weaker than he was. Unease twisted inside Sam as he realized Will would make an easy target, but so too would Nadine. Throwing around accusations wasn't going to help if the woman was trapped in an abusive relationship.

"I'm not saying anything, Nadine. I'm asking. Is everything okay at home? Do you need any help?"

"I'm fine. Everything's fine."

"And Will?" Sam couldn't resist asking.

"That was…an accident."

"Nadine—"

"Please, Sam. Just leave it alone." She rushed off before taking his order, but it was just as well. Sam had lost his appetite.

He wished there was something more he could do, but thanks to his friendship with Billy, Sam knew enough about law enforcement to realize the sheriff would need proof. More than that, he would need Nadine or Will to press charges.

He'd talk to Will again, he decided, and if that didn't work, then maybe he'd have a talk with Darrell Nelson.

The bell over the diner's door rang, and Sam looked up in time to see an already familiar blonde step inside. Kara slid her sunglasses up to the top of her head, pushing her straight hair back from her face. She glanced uncertainly around the crowded diner, and he had the feeling that holding Timmy's hand was giving her as much reassurance as it gave the little boy.

Her nephew. Not her son. Single moms had always been off-limits, and even though something about Kara tempted him to break that rule, he was glad he wouldn't have to. Glad he wouldn't have to look too closely at the reason why he would have been so willing to cross that line.

A hint of weariness seemed to tug at her shoulders, something he hadn't noticed before. She was tired after her trip from—

He frowned. Where, exactly? he wondered, as he realized she hadn't told him where she was from. Or what had brought her to Clearville. Or how long she was staying. True, they hadn't had much chance to talk, but weren't those simple facts ones that normally came up right off the bat?

As Kara paid for a to-go order and reached for the bag, Sam was tempted to cross the diner and offer to carry it for her, like some kid with a crush on a pretty girl, willing to cart around an armload of books if that was what it took to have her smile at him.

She held out her free hand to her nephew, who'd wandered a few feet away to crawl into the booth closest to the front window, but Sam stayed put as the two of them left the diner. No need to push his luck when he could bide his time. After all, he already had a date with the lady the following night.

Thinking he might find out something about the woman who had him so intrigued, he made his way to the front counter. "Hey, Rolly, the blonde who came in for take-out, what did she order?"

"Why is that any of your business?" the other of the diners demanded.

"Give me a break," Sam said, familiar with the older man's soft spot for young women. Kara must have quickly made an impression on Rolly, just as she had on him. "I'm just trying to get an idea of the lady's tastes."

The former army cook eyed Sam as if he'd never seen him before. "Not someone like you."

"Is that right?"

"Sure is."

Certainty rang in the older man's voice, taking some of the fun out of the game. The attraction was mutual, Sam would stake his reputation on that. But even though he'd seen the spark of awareness in Kara's gaze, the slight blush on her cheeks, he also sensed a wariness in her. A deer-in-the-headlights hesitation that warned him she'd be more likely to run away from him than rush into his arms.

"What makes you think a lady like that wouldn't want to go out with me?" he asked Rolly.

"You are something else, Sam." A familiar female voice had him turning to face Debbie Mattson. Judging by the smirk bringing out the dimples in her round cheeks, she'd been standing behind him all along. "All a woman has to do is cross the town line and you start sensing fresh meat."

Annoyance flickered through Sam. Not so much at the baker's pointed barb. That was the kind of relationship they had after knowing each since grade school. It was more the way Debbie had lumped Kara in with all the other women he—okay, he had to admit it—all the women he'd chased after.

He couldn't come close to putting a finger on what made Kara different. But he'd long ago perfected the ability to hide his true feelings. "My radar must be working overtime, seeing as I met Kara even before she hit town."

"You're kidding."

"Nope, met her when she ended up with a flat on the side of the road."

Aware of the narrow mountain roads leading to town and the lack of cell coverage, Debbie's smirk faded some. "She was lucky you happened by."

"That's what I said!"

She rolled her eyes with a laugh. "Why do I have the feeling you're not joking? Honestly, Sam, when the right woman comes along, how is she going to take you seriously?"

Serious relationships led to serious heartache, and that was something he could do without. "My right kind of woman is all about having a good time."

They might just have met, but his first glance had revealed that Kara wasn't the "girls just want to have fun" type. All that meant, though, was that whatever relationship they had wouldn't last, already a guarantee thanks to Kara's temporary status in his hometown. He had nothing to worry about.

"Well, I wish you and your good-time girl good luck," Debbie said as a waitress waved her over to a table she'd just cleared.

Sam doubted Debbie's wishes had much to do with it, but luck was definitely on his side, he decided, as he spotted a furry green leg sticking out from the corner booth. He grinned as he picked up the familiar stuffed dinosaur. It looked like Kara needed rescuing a second time.

Kara collapsed onto the small sofa in the tiny living area of the hotel's two-room suite. Exhaustion pulled at her until she thought she might sink clear through the too-soft navy brocade cushions and never get up again. The two-day drive had taken a lot out of her, but the last half hour had completely worn her out.

How could she have lost Timmy's stuffed animal? It wasn't like she didn't know how much the dinosaur meant to him. Losing that dinosaur, one of the last connections to Marti…it felt like another part of her sister had just slipped away.

As soon as Timmy had climbed into the unfamiliar bed and realized the toy wasn't waiting there for him, they'd searched the minivan, checking between and beneath the seats. She'd tried asking him the last time he remembered having the dinosaur, but Timmy had started to cry, and Kara had been too upset herself to push him harder.

She didn't know what to think about Timmy's last tearful request to sleep with the tiny car Sam had given him. She should have been grateful that the little boy had taken comfort in the toy. But she only felt like that much more of failure, so much so that she wondered if Marti hadn't had the right idea.

Maybe Timmy would be better off with Sam.

A knock on the door pulled her from those heartbreaking thoughts, and Kara wiped her eyes as she pushed off the sofa. The dinosaur would turn up. It had to.

"Who is it?" she called out softly as she reached the white paneled door.

"Room service."

"I didn't…" Her voice trailed off as she recognized the masculine voice and the already too familiar skip in her pulse. *Sam...*

Opening the door without removing the safety chain, she met his gaze through the narrow gap in the door. "I didn't order room service."

"You didn't order dessert at Rolly's either, which is a

real shame because they have the best chocolate silk pie around," he said, holding up a clear plastic container with a huge slice inside.

"You brought—wait, how do you know what I ordered at the diner?"

"I'd stopped in there. You didn't see me, but—"

"You noticed I didn't order dessert," she filled in, "and brought me pie?"

Kara didn't know what to think about Sam making such an effort to see her again. After all, she could hardly tell him she wasn't interested when she'd already asked him out for a date! And she could hardly tell herself she wasn't interested when her racing heartbeat and the heat rising to her cheeks would have labeled her a liar.

"Yep. Figure this way, you'll owe me…dinner and two desserts." He paused as he pretended to tally up her debt.

"What if I don't like pie?"

"Everyone likes pie." Confidence rang in his voice and casual posture, leaning against the side of the recessed doorway, offering up the rich, decadent, tempting dessert. "And then there's always my other special delivery."

Kara gasped as he brought his other hand into sight and quickly slammed the door shut. She slid back the security chain and opened the door all the way to reach out for the stuffed dinosaur Sam held. Sinking her fingers into the soft green fur, she pulled the toy to her chest. "Where did you find him?"

"Timmy left him in the booth at the diner."

"But I called! They said he wasn't there."

Sam flinched a little. "Yeah, that's probably because I'd already taken him with me. I was planning to come straight over here, but then I got a call about a motorist who'd broken down on the highway. Sorry about that."

"You had a job to do. That's more important."

"More important than reptile relocation?"

"Yes," she said with a laugh at his teasing. "You know how these stuffed dinosaurs make nuisances of themselves in urban areas."

"We're lucky he didn't destroy Tokyo. He'll be much happier in his natural habitat."

"Timmy will be thrilled to have him back. Thank you, Sam." Kara dropped her gaze, mortified to feel the sting of tears burning her eyes.

He'd brought back a stuffed animal, not a lost child….

"Hey, are you okay?"

Blinking quickly, Kara glanced up to find Sam watching her, concern creasing his forehead. It was the first time she'd seen him without his charmer's smile. A shield, she realized suddenly, for his true feelings. It was enough to make her wonder if he was the carefree womanizer she'd immediately pegged him as. If he might be so much more than he let people see.

"I, um, I'm fine. It's just been a long few days." Curiosity had his green eyes narrowing, and Kara's pulse took a slightly panicked leap. She wasn't a good liar. She prided herself on being honest by nature. But she wasn't ready to tell the whole truth.

She hugged the dinosaur tighter to her chest. Nowhere near ready.

"Hey, look, it's getting late, so why don't I head out?"

She should let him go. He was offering, so all she had to do was thank him again and send him on his way….

But instead, she heard herself say, "I always have liked chocolate silk pie."

Sam grinned as if he'd known that all along. "The pie is a given, but my staying doesn't have to be."

"No, please stay," she said as she stepped back to let him into the small living area of the room.

It was better this way, Kara told herself even as Sam opened the container and removed two plastic forks—a sign he'd hoped to share her dessert all along. She wanted to get to know him and it might be easier in this casual setting rather than trying to learn everything she could on their date.

But what questions could she ask that would determine whether or not Sam would make a good father? And how was she supposed to decide what answers would be right or wrong?

Past mistakes proved she wasn't the best authority when it came to judging a man's character. What if she trusted Sam to be a good guy, to do the right thing where Timmy was concerned? And what if she was wrong?

Unlike her previous relationship, this time it wasn't her trust that would be betrayed, her heart that would be broken. This time, Timmy's future was at stake.

Hoping she could pull this interrogation off without gaining Sam's suspicion instead of his confidence, she settled back on the sofa. The piece of furniture seemed so much smaller now with Sam taking up the second cushion. His booted feet rested on the floor, his muscular, denim-clad thighs spread wide as he leaned forward and dug his fork into the piece of pie.

He leaned back, his shoulders angled toward her as he held out the fork. "You get first bite. Only fair since I bought it for you."

The crisp, buttery crust and rich chocolate filling melted on her tongue, but it was the heat in Sam's eyes as her lips closed over the plastic fork that made Kara feel like she was dissolving. Everything from her willpower and determination to keep Sam at a distance, to the future she pictured for herself and Timmy, was disappearing like sugar in water. Soon there'd be nothing left.

Pulling back quickly, she busied herself reaching for a napkin and her own fork. "It's, uh, very good. Thank you," she said, clearing her throat to get the words past the lump of chocolate-coated desire lodged there. "You said before that Clearville's your hometown, right?" Striving for a casual, let's-get-to-know-each-other tone, she added, "Tell me what it was like growing up here."

Marti had once laughed at her nervousness on first dates. "Dating's a piece of cake," her sister insisted. "Guys love to talk about themselves. All you have to do is pretend you're interested."

But as Sam talked about his childhood in the small community, Kara didn't have to pretend. He was great storyteller, and she was reluctantly fascinated at his antics as the youngest son with two big brothers who were as likely to stick up for him as they were to knock him down.

"Not that I didn't deserve it," he reassured her with a grin, the closeness he shared with Nick and Drew and his little sister, Sophia, evident in his tone of voice. And his parents…Kara didn't think she'd ever met anyone who spoke with more love and respect for his parents.

Not once did he mention his parents using the natural rivalry that could exist between siblings to make them try harder or push themselves further. Not as her parents had with her and Marti.

"Sorry, I think I've bored you with stories about my family long enough. I've monopolized the conversation without giving you a turn."

A turn to talk about her family. About Marti….

She couldn't do it. She couldn't look Sam in the eye and talk about her sister as if she was someone he didn't know. As a stranger instead of the mother of his child and someone he might have cared about. Might have loved.

"I'm sorry, Sam," she said as she rose to her feet, "but

I really am tired. Maybe—maybe we can talk about my family some other time?"

"Sure. I stayed longer than I planned. I wanted to drop off the dinosaur and the dessert, not put you to sleep with talk about my family."

"You didn't put me to sleep." And as tired as she was, Kara doubted she'd find a peaceful night's rest anytime soon. Not when she pictured Sam as a young boy, looking very much like Timmy did now, tagging along after his big brothers, teasing his little sister, growing up in a small town where anyone would want to raise their child….

Maybe even a town where Marti had wanted Sam to raise Timmy.

Reaching the door, Sam turned back to face her. "So tomorrow night then?"

"Right. Dinner and two desserts."

"Oh, I get it," he grinned. "You think you can pay me back and be done with me after one night, but it's not going to be that easy."

Kara knew what was easy—getting pulled in by Sam's smile. By the warmth in his eyes that called to her like a light left on in a front window, ready to embrace and welcome her home. His teasing expression encouraged her to kick back, relax, take a load off….

For one crazy second, she thought about telling him the truth right then and there. Unloading the burden that had been dragging her down, resting her head on his broad shoulder and hearing him say everything would be okay. But the last time she'd put her trust in a man, her hope and her heart had been trampled. She couldn't trust Sam, not yet.

But neither could she resist his invitation to join in the fun. "Don't tell me, you plan to play hard to get?"

"You better believe it. Tomorrow night, I figure it'll

be drinks and appetizers. Then our next date, we'll have drinks and appetizers. And for our third date—"

"Let me guess—drinks and appetizers?"

"Nah, by our third date, I figure we'll be ready for the main course."

Kara swallowed. Were they still talking about food? The heat in Sam's gaze seemed to be saying so much more, but her heart was pounding so loudly she couldn't think over the sound. She couldn't think at all as he stepped closer and threaded his fingers through her hair. "Sam—"

Her lips were already parted on the whisper of his name, already parted for his kiss—a kiss that brushed across her cheek. "Better not spoil our appetites," he murmured before wishing her goodnight and leaving before Kara had the chance to recover or respond.

Chapter Four

Sam had never been the jealous type, but arriving at Kara's hotel room the next evening and realizing she was ready to stand him up for another guy didn't sit well. Not even if the other guy was only about three and a half feet tall.

She'd looked adorably flustered as she opened the door. Much as she had the previous night when he'd taken off without giving her the kiss she'd expected—and the one he'd craved. Gazing down at her as her eyes widened with an awakening hunger after all that talk about appetizers and main courses, it had taken more willpower than he thought he possessed to touch her cheek with his lips. And even then the scent and softness of her skin had sent a rush of desire speeding through his veins, a response totally out of proportion for such a chaste kiss.

With any other woman, he wouldn't have stopped there, not when he was ready to race toward the finish line. But the vulnerability Kara tried so hard to hide brought out a protective streak in him that gave him the strength to pull back. She was the type of woman who made a man want to take things slow. Made *him* want to take things slow.

"I thought I'd be ready to go by now," she said as he followed her into the suite. Her feet were bare, showing off toes painted a color that reminded him of ripe raspberries, and her yellow silk shirt was untucked in back. "But Timmy wanted a snack before bed."

Sam didn't see her nephew, but the kid had left a trail of breadcrumbs. The bright orange remains of cheesy goldfish crackers dusted the coffee table, beside an empty bottle that had once held grape juice, judging by the small purplish flecks on Kara's cream-colored pants. "The babysitter won't be here for another fifteen minutes, so you have plenty of time to change."

"Change?" She followed his gaze and made a soft sound beneath her breath as she brushed uselessly at her pants. "I should check on Timmy." She glanced back over her shoulder at the closed bathroom door. "He's supposed to be brushing his teeth, but by now he's probably flooded the bathroom. I'm sorry, Sam."

He heard the *but* coming from miles away and stopped the word the best way he could. Cupping her hands in his face, he caught her gasp against his lips, tasting the sweetness of her surprise and stopping there. It was one thing to steal a quick kiss; he wouldn't take more. Not without some sign from Kara. His heart thundered with anticipation. Waiting…wanting…

Kara's pulse leaped beneath his fingertips, and the knowledge that she was just as affected made pulling away impossible, but he still waited. With another small sound, she parted her lips beneath his, and Sam deepened the kiss. His tongue stroked hers, and a delicious shiver shook her entire body. He reveled in the telling reaction, and he had to have more. He pulled her body closer to his, his fingers instinctively finding the small gap between her shirttail and her skirt and discovering skin smoother than silk beneath. Her fingers tangled in his hair, and he had the crazy thought that this wasn't what a first kiss was supposed to be like.

A first kiss was supposed to be a tease, a promise of more to come, like the brush of his lips against her cheek the night before, but this kiss—*this* kiss delivered an instant rush of desire that was enough to make him want to forget about everything but the woman in his arms. Everything including the little boy in the other room and the very sharp, very nosy babysitter already on her way.

Sam wasn't sure how, but he forced himself to pull away and meet Kara's startled gaze. Her eyes were wide and a flush of color lit her cheeks. One look at her lips and anyone would know he'd kissed her. Sam swallowed and dragged his gaze away. One more look and he'd be kissing her again.

"What, um, was that for?"

"Unless I'm totally off my game," he said, struggling to find his typical teasing tone, "this date is about to come to an end. Seemed like the right time for a goodnight kiss."

Kara flushed a brighter shade of red, but before she could respond, Timmy's voice drifted out from the bathroom. A moment later he appeared in the hallway and stopped short as he caught sight of Sam.

Despite the interruption, Sam couldn't help the small grin that tugged at his lips. Judging by the pale blue foam circling the boy's mouth, Timmy had used half a tube of toothpaste to brush his teeth, and Sam could only imagine the mess left behind. He wore a pair of red pajamas with a fierce-looking T-Rex emblazoned on the chest. Fresh from a bath, his damp hair formed a halo of blond ringlets.

Poor guy. As a kid, he'd had hair just like that and man, had he hated those "girly" curls. Or at least he had until he learned to appreciate having a woman run her fingers through them....

Cutting off that thought, Sam said, "Hey, Timmy. I brought you something." He reached into his pants' pocket and pulled out a miniature tow truck. Aware of Kara standing behind him, he knelt down in front of the little boy and handed him the toy. "That other car you picked out looks like the one I drive, but I have a tow truck, too."

"Like this one?"

"Yep. And now you have a sports car and a tow truck."

"Just like you?"

"Just like me."

Kara made a small sound, and Sam glanced over his shoulder to find her watching closely. An air of expectation hovered between them as their eyes met, as if she were holding her breath and waiting for him to—he didn't know what. Sam pushed to his feet but before he had a chance to say anything, she brushed by him.

"I better go change."

"Are you sure you still want to go?" As reluctant as he was to give Kara an easy out, something felt off. For a brief moment when he'd held her in his arms, she'd let down her guard. She'd kissed him back with enough unfiltered desire to let him know the attraction wasn't one-sided. But now the warmth in her caramel eyes had hardened with a reluctance and wariness he didn't understand.

Some of the tension eased as she lowered her arm from across her chest. The locket she'd been clutching like a protective amulet slipped back beneath the shallow V of her pale yellow shirt. "I'm sure. I'll just be a minute."

"Take your time," Sam said, but Kara closed the bedroom door on the last word, disappearing inside and leaving him alone with Timmy.

The little boy was gazing down at the miniature tow

truck, slowly spinning one of the back tires with his index finger. Finally, he looked up shyly and asked, "Is the tow truck fast like your red car?"

"Not as fast as the car." Wondering if Timmy was still trying to outrun those monsters, he added, "But the thing about a truck is that it has a diesel engine that's really loud. Loud enough to hear from miles away so everybody knows it's coming and gets outta the way."

Timmy thought about that for a moment before saying, "I like the fast car better."

"Me, too, but why don't you keep the tow truck anyway."

"What do you say, Timmy?"

Sam looked up at the sound of Kara's voice. She'd changed her entire outfit, replacing the stained off-white pants and silk blouse with a navy blue dress. He mentally gave Timmy a high five for spilling his juice. The dress wasn't showy, with its short sleeves and modest neckline trimmed with white fabric, but the knee-length skirt left Kara's legs bare. She'd swept her hair back into a low ponytail and had touched up her lip gloss, too, replacing a bit of the shine he'd wiped away with his kiss. Which only made him want to kiss her again….

He wondered how long she'd been watching from the bedroom doorway and at the mix of emotions behind her eyes. He thought he'd done okay in his talk with Timmy, and yet, instead of looking pleased, she almost looked… worried.

"Thanks, Sam."

She smiled at her nephew's show of manners, and whatever Sam saw or thought he saw was gone. A knock sounded at the door, and Sam greeted Hope Daniels with a hug.

Curiosity gleamed from behind her wire-rimmed glasses

as he introduced her to Kara. "So nice to meet you, dear. And this must be…Timmy?"

The little boy had ducked behind Kara's skirt at Hope's arrival but peeked out to stare at the older woman like she was some kind of fairy godmother. With her long silver-streaked hair, floral skirt and flowing blouse, she could almost fit the bill.

Hope inhaled softly as she caught sight of the little boy. "Well, look at you."

Sam smiled. Hope had always had a soft spot for kids. He thought she'd always had a soft spot for him, too, so the frown she shot his way took him by surprise.

Hope knew he didn't normally date women with kids. Did she think he was in over his head? If he could, he would have assured her he knew what he was doing. Any relationship with Kara had a built-in expiration date. He wanted to see Kara for as long as she was in town, but once she left for home, that was it.

Game over.

But as he reached out to take Kara's hand, the quickening beat of his heart made him wonder if the rules hadn't already changed.

I can do this, Kara repeated the reminder as Sam led her along the brick walkway cutting across the hotel's lush green lawn. *I just have to stay focused.*

She needed to find out the kind of man Sam Pirelli was. To learn what kind of father he might be. To know without a doubt how amazing it felt to be held in his arms….

Kara stumbled slightly as the brick pavers gave way to asphalt in the parking lot. Sam reached out, wrapping a muscled arm around her and pulling her back against his chest.

"Careful," he murmured.

Shivers danced along her spine at the brush of his lips and his breath against her ear, and Kara hazarded a glance over her shoulder. A dangerous move that brought those lips mere inches from her own.

Oh, yes, she had to be very careful.

Tonight Sam had replaced his usual jeans and T-shirt with a pair of neatly pressed khaki pants and a button-down shirt. The soft blue fabric did amazing things to his green eyes and brought to mind the glorious combination of the blue sky above towering pines.

She'd been right in believing when it came to Sam clothes didn't make the man, but he *did* look good. Good enough to steal her breath and scatter her thoughts. Something she couldn't allow with Timmy's future—with *her* future—at stake.

"Um, thank you," she said as she eased away, only to immediately miss the warmth of his arm around her.

Sam gazed down at her, and for a split second, Kara worried he was going to question her reasons for drawing away. Or worse, pull her back into his arms where she feared she wouldn't have the willpower to resist a second time.

But he merely took her hand and led her across the parking lot. "I thought we could go to the Clearville Bar and Grille. The food's good, and there's a live band tonight." He turned to face her as they reached the Corvette, his gaze sweeping her from head to toe with a look of complete male appreciation.

"Or maybe the Sand Dollar Inn. It's where all the locals go for special occasions—birthdays, anniversaries, engagements…" His voice trailed away for a moment before he shook off an old memory. "I just realized I haven't set foot in that place since my senior prom."

Despite the easy laugh, Kara sensed he'd just as soon never set foot in the restaurant again. And although she'd never heard of the Sand Dollar Inn, she could already picture it—fresh-cut flowers in tiny vases, elegantly patterned place settings and rich tablecloths. A place with a quiet, intimate, romantic atmosphere and not at all somewhere she should be with Sam Pirelli.

"No, really, the Bar and Grille sounds fun."

"Good." Sam's smile was relieved enough to make Kara wonder what had happened on that prom night, but digging into his ancient history would be going too far.

"It's just down the street, isn't it?" She'd feel better about leaving Timmy knowing that she was only a block or two away.

"That's right. You know, my family has known Hope for years. She owns the antique shop in town but recently hired my sister to run the place." He reached out to open the passenger door.

"She seems like quite the character."

"Oh, she is. But you don't have to worry. Timmy's in good hands."

Kara had never put much stock in the power of suggestion, but the mere mention of being in safe hands was enough to make her gaze drop to the wide palm he'd braced on the top of the open door. Against her will, her imagination leaped to the memory of that same hand pressing into her flesh…

"And this is Clearville, so no matter where we go, we won't be more than fifteen minutes away."

Realizing Sam had picked up on her concern, she gave a slightly self-conscious laugh. "You probably think I'm being ridiculous."

"Not at all. I think you're a very caring aunt."

Curiosity lingered in his expression, and Kara knew he wondered why she was the one taking care of Timmy. Nerves gripped her stomach. The longer she put off telling

Sam the truth, the harder it would be when she told him. *If* she told him....

Unable to meet his gaze, she turned to the open door. "There's no backseat."

Sam's deep chuckle danced down her spine like a playful caress even as embarrassed heat flooded her cheeks. No backseat? Did she have to make it sound like she wanted to crawl in the back for a make-out session?

"Nope. We'll just have to keep our hands to ourselves. It's gonna be tough, I know."

Turning to face him, she argued, "I didn't mean that. I just meant—"

A two-seater hot rod didn't have room for a child's booster seat in the back. It was a bachelor's car. Not the kind of vehicle that spoke of responsibility or safety. A ride that, instead, screamed freedom and speed, one that was fast enough to outrun the monsters in a four-year-old's mind.

Memory of the big man crouched down in front of the little boy replayed in Kara's mind, weakening her resolve. He was good with Timmy. Kind and patient and thoughtful. Try as she might, she couldn't deny *that*.

"It doesn't seem very...practical," she finished lamely as she ducked into the passenger seat.

Sam was still chuckling as he slid behind the wheel and turned the key. The engine jumped to life, and Kara sensed the power and speed beneath the hood, but Sam controlled both with ease as he pulled out of the lot and drove the small town speed limit. Taking his time...the same way he had with their kiss.

Heat rose in her cheeks, and she had to force herself to listen to what he was saying. "You're right. Most guys buy a car like this because it's cool or powerful or because girls dig it."

"I guess I'm not like most girls."

"And I'm not most guys."

"So you didn't buy the car because it's cool and powerful and girls dig it?"

"Nope. My reasons were far more..." Glancing over, he winked. "Practical."

Kara couldn't help but give a small and disbelieving laugh. "Really?"

"Yep. This car was in pretty bad shape, but I could see her potential."

"Her?"

"Anything this gorgeous has to be female."

"If you say so."

"Jealous?" he teased.

"Please," Kara scoffed. "So you bought this pile of junk—"

"Hey, watch how you talk about my girl here!" Sam patted the wheel as if soothing the car's feelings before continuing. "I knew once I fixed her up I could sell her at a car auction."

She shot him a curious glance. "I've seen some of those auctions advertised on television."

"The first one I went to, I was working for a rich old guy who used to live here in Clearville part-time. He didn't like to fly, so he would drive from back east in this amazing Rolls-Royce. One year, he had some engine trouble. He was ready to fly his own mechanic out when someone gave him my name. He took one look at me, and I didn't think I had a chance of getting my hands on that car."

"How did you change his mind?"

"I told him if he wasn't happy with the job I did, I'd fly his mechanic out to fix the car."

"I'm guessing that wasn't necessary."

"Nope. I got that baby up and running, and after that,

we spent hours talking cars. He told me he wanted to invest in another classic and asked if I'd be willing to work an auction for him, to pick out the cars I thought were the best deals and make a bid for him." Sam shot a grin her way. "I spent over three-hundred grand on a sixty-year-old Mercedes-Benz."

His grin turned into a full laugh when Kara's jaw dropped. "That's crazy!"

"Yeah, but it sure was fun." Even after five years, Sam still remembered the air of excitement and anticipation as the bids rose higher and higher until all other competition fell away. It hadn't even mattered that the money and the car weren't his. And the attention that came with making the winning offer hadn't hurt either, he admitted to himself, remembering the curvy blonde who'd caught his eye and the heated two-week fling that followed.

At first, they'd exchanged phone calls and emails. But after a month or so, the calls and texts had dwindled away. He figured the reality of a long-distance relationship with a small-town mechanic wasn't as exciting as a fantasy getaway with a guy on a millionaire's payroll.

Pushing thoughts of the other woman into the past where they belonged, he glanced over at Kara. "Malcolm's health isn't good enough for him to come out anymore. And even though I only had a chance to work on his cars for a few months, it was enough to show me what I really wanted to do. This beauty may be my first, but she won't be my last. As soon as I finish her paint job, I'll start taking her to auctions, see what I can get for her and find another classic to fix up."

"What about your garage? I mean, you have a business to run."

"Will's been asking for more hours lately. I figure if I

hire on another part-time mechanic, that should cover the days when I'm out of town."

"You sound pretty excited."

"I am. This baby's going to give me the chance to do more than everyday oil changes. I'll finally be able to focus on restoring classic cars as more than just a side job."

"That's important, isn't it? To follow your dream?"

Sam wasn't sure how it happened, but once again, their conversation was centering around him, and he had to ask, "Have you followed yours?"

She hesitated just briefly before saying, "I did. I always wanted to be a teacher."

"What grade do you teach?"

"College, actually. English Lit."

He shouldn't have been surprised. From the first, Kara had struck him as intelligent and well-educated. She had loved school enough to make teaching at the highest level her profession while his only dreams about school had centered around the day he could escape and never go back.

"So," he teased as his defenses from those school days kicked in. "Does that mean I should call you Professor?"

"Only if you sign up for one of my advanced literature classes."

Yeah, Sam didn't see that happening. But there was something else he didn't see happening either. No reason to worry about the miles that separated where they lived.

Not when their lives were worlds apart.

Walking into the rustic bar with Sam, Kara immediately saw what it would be like to hang out with a minor celebrity. In a town the size of Clearville, she supposed it wasn't uncommon for everyone to know everyone else, but she hadn't expected half-a-dozen or so people to stop him for a handshake or high five.

"Hey, Sam! Good to see you. Don't forget, I owe you a beer for checking out that car for Cindy," a man in his fifties with salt-and-pepper hair called out from his seat at the bar.

"You don't owe me for that. Besides, I doubt Cindy thinks I did her much of a favor."

"She's sixteen years old," the man argued with a father's exasperation. "She needs a car that's reliable."

"I know, but it was a nice-looking car."

"Yeah, and she would have looked great standing next to it when the engine gave out in the middle of nowhere."

"Let me know if she finds another one. I'd be glad to take a look."

"That was nice of you," Kara said as he guided her toward a table away from the dance floor and the area where the band was setting up.

"I was doing a favor for a friend. No big deal," he said as he took his seat and leaned back in the chair.

Like his posture, his statement was relaxed and comfortable with no sense of pretension or false modesty. Maybe it was all part of small town mentality of neighbor helping neighbor, or maybe it was just…Sam.

He fit so well. Maybe that was why his plans to spend so much time away from Clearville had taken her by surprise. But that was a good thing, right? Hauling classic cars to shows all over the country didn't fit with raising a young son. Wouldn't it make so much more sense for Timmy to live with *her* and Sam could visit whenever his travels brought him south?

For the first time since reading Marti's letter, a small seed of hope started to bloom inside her.

A short-skirted waitress swung by with ice water and menus. Kara barely had a chance to glance inside when a feminine voice called out Sam's name. She looked up and recognized the brunette who'd brought Sam lunch the day before.

"I didn't expect to see you here." The woman's dark brows winged upward when she caught sight of Kara, and Sam gave a faint groan.

"This is a part of small-town life I didn't get a chance to warn you about. No matter where you go or what you do, you'll end up seeing somebody you know."

Someone like a girlfriend who wasn't supposed to know Sam was on a date with another woman?

The thought was enough to make Kara want to duck beneath the tablecloth. But then irritation overcame embarrassment as Sam rose and met the other woman with a wide, unrepentant grin. "Fifi!"

If he was the least bit ashamed at getting caught red-handed, he didn't show it. He greeted the brunette with a one-armed hug, and even though the petite woman slapped his arm, the blow wasn't the least bit serious.

"How many times have I told you not to call me that?" she demanded.

"Sorry." Sam grinned unapologetically before adding, "Sophia."

As in his sister Sophia? Only then did Kara spot the dark-haired man gazing at the other woman with a look of—well, Kara wasn't sure she'd ever seen a man look at a woman with such love and tenderness and pride. And when Sophia glanced over her shoulder to return his gaze, Kara thought she knew what Sam meant about not having enough privacy. After witnessing that personal exchange, she felt like she'd been spying on an intimate moment.

"Kara, this is my sister, Sophia, and my new brother-in-law, Jake Cameron."

Jake slid an arm around his wife, and Kara saw what she'd missed from a distance. The red-and-white summer dress with its ruffled bodice and high waistline loosely draped Sophia's petite frame, but up close her rounded belly was more obvious.

Sam's sister was pregnant.

Painful memories closed in—shadows creeping near as light disappeared—but Kara shoved them back. Her fingers itched to reach for the locket around her neck, but she hid them in her lap beneath the table.

Forcing a smile, she said, "It's nice to meet you both."

"You, too. I don't think I've seen you around."

Kara sensed Sam's exasperation as his sister pulled out a free chair and made herself comfortable, but he merely passed his brother-in-law a wry look and a menu before sitting back down. "Why don't you join us, Sophia?"

"We will, Sam," she shot back tartly.

A small smile tugged at Kara's lips. The antagonism and affection between the siblings reminded her of her relationship with Marti. Oh, how she missed that…missed her sister! But the warmth of family and fun kept the cold feeling of sorrow at bay.

See? Marti's voice seemed to whisper. *See why I brought you here?*

The conversation moved on to the best the restaurant had to offer and before long, the group had decided on their meals—burgers for the men and salads for the women.

"So, how did you two meet?" Sophia asked once the waitress had taken their orders.

"I was stuck on the side of the road with a flat tire and no cell service, and Sam rescued me." She'd meant the comment to come out as a light tease, mocking the way he seemed to think he could sweep her off her feet—at that first meeting and, well, every time their paths had crossed since. Somehow, though, the words didn't come out that way, sounding far more romantic and, heaven help her, love struck than she intended.

Sam's eyes darkened as he met her gaze, and Kara had the feeling that if Sophia and Jake weren't sitting at the table, he would have kissed her again.

"That's my brother," Sophia said with a fond smile. "He has always had a thing for rescuing damsels in distress."

Easing back in her chair a little under Sam's knowing gaze—as if a few inches would be a safe enough distance to void the attraction between them—Kara argued, "I wouldn't say I was in distress."

"Are you kidding?" Picking up where she'd left off and embellishing greatly, he said, "There you were, trapped on the edge of wilderness, miles from civilization, monsters closing in on every side…"

"Monsters?" Jake echoed. "Exactly where did you break down?"

"Just outside of town and the monsters—that was my nephew's imagination."

"How old is your nephew?" Sophia asked.

"He's just turned four, and he has a big imagination. Monster-sized, I suppose you could say."

"Oh, that's a great age, isn't it?"

The brunette rested her hands expectantly on her belly, and Kara knew the questions she was supposed to ask. The polite interest she was supposed to show. Sophia certainly wasn't the first pregnant woman Kara had run into over the last twelve years. So why did the questions seem so much harder to ask?

"When are you due?"

"Not soon enough! But I'm not due for another four months."

No, please, it's too soon! I'm not due for months…

"Babies are wonderful," Sophia was saying, but her

voice sounded far away—on the other side of Kara's memories. "So cute and cuddly with those chubby cheeks, you just want to squeeze them. I'm afraid I'm going to spoil this baby rotten."

Cute. Cuddly. Chubby cheeks.

Yes, Kara knew that was how babies were supposed to look. How many times had she passed by the hospital nursery, staring with such longing, such envy at those cute, cuddly, *healthy* babies until she simply couldn't take it anymore?

"Kara?" Sam voice, soft and warm, cut into those hard, cold memories. "Are you okay?"

The table and restaurant snapped back into focus and she met Sam's concerned gaze. "I'm fine. I— Do you know what you're having?" she asked, feeling like she was walking by the nursery all over again, torturing herself with this conversation.

This isn't about you, she reminded herself as she met Sophia's once-again smiling face. *Sophia and Jake are going to have that happy, healthy baby, and it has nothing to do with you.*

"We asked the doctor not to tell, but both Jake and I believe it's going to be a little boy."

"Here's hoping," Sam said, lifting a glass toward Jake.

"What's wrong with girls?" Sophia demanded.

"Girls are trouble. You worry way more about them than you do about boys."

Sophia looked over at her husband. "Don't tell me you buy into that theory, too."

"Sorry, sweetheart. I'd argue the trouble part, but I think there's less to worry about with sons than daughters."

"Right. Because guys are so tough, especially with macho-men dads like the two of you would be."

"That's right," Sam agreed with a fist bump to Jake who

seemed to return the gesture with more amusement than agreement. "Besides, if you have a boy, think of all the guy things you get to do—play football, go fishing, teach them how to fix cars…"

Now's your chance. You can ask him any question you want about being a father, raising a son, and no one will question your reasons for asking.

But the words stayed stuck in Kara's throat, caught there, maybe, by the declarations Sam had already made? Guys were supposed to be tough, macho. They were supposed to like trucks and sports and roughhousing. They weren't supposed to be shy, imaginative souls. They weren't supposed to be like Timmy.

If Sam knew the boy was his son, would he set out to toughen him up? Would he try to wear away the boy's sensitive spirit?

She couldn't let that happen. She *wouldn't* let that happen.

Chapter Five

"Sorry about my family crashing our date," Sam said once Sophia and Jake had left for the evening. As much as he loved his sister, a double date had not been part of his plans.

Kara swirled a straw through the diet soda she'd been nursing. "You talk a lot about your family. It was…good to meet them."

"I know they both got a kick out of you trying to pay for my meal."

"Well, I do owe you, remember?"

"Maybe next time," he said lightly, even though he couldn't quite get a feel for Kara's thoughts about *this* time.

She'd joined in, taking Sophia's side during his teasing verbal battles with his sister. The two of them seemed to hit it off, but then the talk had turned to babies and kids, and Kara had withdrawn. She'd fallen silent as he'd joked with Sophia about having a boy—

Aw, hell…

How'd he miss that? Kara didn't have any kids, but he'd already seen how protective she was of Timmy. A boy who was not, Sam had to admit, the toughest of little guys.

"That stuff I said about raising boys, well, I was just giving Sophia a hard time. That's what big brothers do."

"Like your brothers did to you?"

"You bet. But they looked out for me, too. The way you look out for Timmy."

Her gaze dropped to the glass in her hand. "I know Timmy isn't what you'd consider tough. But he's a sweet boy, Sam. A really great kid."

Kara looked up then, a wealth of emotion in her eyes as if she expected him to argue. Or as if what he thought mattered. "Sure he is. Anybody can see that."

"He's smart, too. He's already reading and is advanced far beyond most kids his age."

Sam didn't figure that would score too many points for the kid on the playground, but who was he to argue? And no surprise that Kara would place a high value on intelligence. He wondered what she thought of him—all brawn and no brains?

"He probably takes after you."

Kara shook her head. "My sister was incredibly smart. And incredibly beautiful," she added with a quiet wistfulness as if she envied her sister, but Sam didn't see how that could even be possible. Kara had a classic beauty, but when she let down her guard—such as when she talked about her nephew—in those moments, Sam thought she was the most breathtaking woman he'd ever seen.

Her caramel eyes glowed with a warmth that one moment was soft and sweet and in the next was hard as forged steel. She loved Timmy, but she was fiercely protective, as well.

Lost in his thoughts, he nearly missed the words she'd said. Or more to the point, the tense she'd used. "Was," he murmured gently. "You said your sister was smart and beautiful."

Her features grew strained, tension in her shoulders pulling tight on the narrow fingers gripping her glass, and he wished he'd kept his mouth shut. "Ma—my sister died a month ago."

"Do you want to talk—"

Shaking her head almost violently, she lifted her drink and took a quick sip. "No. I—I can't. I can't talk to you..."

It was stupid, Sam told himself, to feel hurt by her withdrawal. They were little more than strangers, only having met the day before, and Kara had no reason to think she'd be able to trust him with her emotions. Hell, he knew better than anyone that he was the good-time guy and not somebody friends or family turned to in a time of need.

"I'm sorry, Kara." The words rang hollow, seeming to emphasize his inadequacy when it came to knowing how to express the empathy he felt. He wasn't sure how things had gotten so deep that he was in over his head on a first date, but he longed to make his way back to shallower ground, to a place where he could once again find his footing.

He'd be better off quitting while he was behind, but then Kara ducked her head and reached for the napkin. Without thinking, Sam beat her to it. Her startled, damp gaze shot to his as he lifted the small white square and dabbed at the tears on her cheeks. His fingertips tingled with a desire to feel her soft, smooth skin against his rough, callused hands, but he kept the napkin between them. At least he did until Kara reached up and covered his hand with her own.

He'd leaned close enough that he could see the faint blush in her cheeks, close enough that he could hear the slight catch in her breathing. He couldn't remember a time when he'd felt so in tune with a woman. He felt the heat rise in his own skin, the breath stall in his own lungs.

It was crazy. He'd chased after too many women for a simple touch to strike him as so different and new. But there was nothing simple about the way touching Kara made him feel.

"Sam, I have to tell you—" Kara's words cut off with a gasp when a man stumbled against her chair, nearly knocking her over.

"Hey, buddy, watch where you're going," Sam advised as he reached out to steady Kara's chair, more worried about her than the clumsy drunk who'd knocked into her.

"Well, if it isn't little Sammy Pirelli."

Sam hadn't been little in a long time, but Darrell Nelson had always been big. A big bully with an even bigger mouth. Looking up to see the burly trucker swaying on his feet, Sam advised, "Darrell, I think it's time for you to head home."

Home to Nadine Gentry and Will…

Damn, he wished he could do something about that, but with Will not talking and Nadine protecting her boyfriend, he didn't know what he could do.

"Not before I meet your new friend." Darrell clamped a beefy hand on a free chair, spun it around and straddled the seat. He braced his arms on the back rungs and leaned close to Kara. "Name's Darrell Nelson. Sammy and I go way back. Did he tell you that?"

Keeping her composure better than Sam would have imagined, Kara said, "I'm relatively certain he's never mentioned you."

"Well, then let me tell you. Me and Sammy, we're real close. So close that when he sticks his nose into my business, I just gotta return the favor, you know?"

He lifted a hand toward her hair, but Sam had had

enough. He shot out of his chair and lifted Darrell to his feet before he could touch one perfect strand. Leaning close enough to smell the stench of beer, he warned the other man, "You're done here, Nelson. And if I see so much as one scratch on Will or Nadine, you'll be done. Period."

Sam unclenched his fists from the front of Darrell's T-shirt, but he should have known it wouldn't be that easy. The cheap shot to his gut would have brought him to his knees if Darrell hadn't been too drunk on his feet to make full contact. Sam didn't have that problem. Using the other man's unsteady momentum, he dropped him to the floor.

Kara stared in horror at the two men wrestling on the ground as diners from the surrounding tables rushed forward to see what was going on.

It had all happened so fast. One minute the two men were talking—well, taunting each other. The next thing she knew, Sam had dodged a punch, grabbed the other man's arm and shoved him to the floor. The excited crowd gave a collective groan when something—a fist, elbow, *skull*—cracked against the hardwood.

"Enough!" A shout rose above the din as the bartender circled the bar, shoving patrons aside to get to where Sam pinned Darrell to the ground. "Seriously, Sam? How many times do I have to tell you Pirellis to keep the fights outta my bar? This is the second time in less than a month—"

"Oh, come on, George!" Kara heard Sam protest as he pushed to his feet and rubbed a knuckle across the corner of his mouth. "That wasn't even me! That was Nick and Travis Parker."

"I don't care! The sheriff can straighten it out this time."

Kara wasn't sure how she eased through the curious bystanders gathered around the two men, but the excited buzz followed. *Bar fights...calls to the sheriff...how many times...*

Only once she stepped outside into the cool night air did she realize the she wasn't hearing the voices from crowd but the ones echoing inside her head.

She'd never witnessed a fight before. A flash of lights down the street signaled the sheriff's imminent arrival, and she quickened her pace. She'd never had any involvement with the police before—not even so much as a parking ticket.

"Kara, wait!" Footsteps pounded behind her, and Sam reached her before she reached the corner. The streetlight illuminated the regret carving grooves in his forehead. "I am so sorry. This is not how I pictured tonight ending."

Car doors slammed behind them, and he glanced back with a muttered curse. "Just—give me a second chance, okay?"

"That's not necessary and...I won't be in town for long."

"Please, Kara." Urgency deepened his voice and threatened to slip beneath her defenses. "When Darrell tried to touch you—I didn't want him laying a hand on you, not after what he did to Will."

"Will?" She sucked in a breath as she remembered the teen's black eye. "Darrell's been abusing Will?"

Sam nodded. "His mother, too, I think. Not that either of them will admit it. Forget pressing charges. But maybe I can for that first punch he threw. It's not much, but it'll keep him from going home drunk tonight."

Kara swallowed the bitter taste of shame. She'd wanted to blame Sam for the fight—for being a hothead who went around proving his toughness by getting into bar brawls. But the concern in his gaze was too honest, too real, for her to ignore.

He was as big and as strong as Darrell Nelson, but Sam

used that strength to protect those who were smaller and weaker. Sam hadn't just been defending her—he'd been protecting Will, too. It was an instinct Kara sensed ran deep—much deeper than the easy smile and teasing attitude he revealed to the rest of the world. Sam was a man who cared deeply. Deeply enough not to let it show. Attraction burned brighter along with a growing admiration, and Kara reached up to brush her fingertips over a scrape on his jaw. "You need to go back and talk to the sheriff."

Catching her wrist, he brought her hand to his mouth. "One more chance." He spoke the words against her fingers, further weakening her resolve.

"Sam…"

A masculine shout from down the street echoed her tremulous whisper, and she slipped her hands from his as Sam looked back. The sheriff pointed at Sam and motioned him over.

"You need to go," Kara repeated.

His shoulders rose and fell on a defeated sigh. "Okay. But I'm taking you to the hotel first." Cutting off her protest, he added, "It's going to take more than a fight with Darrell Nelson to keep me from seeing a lady back to her door."

Hope Daniels looked up from the magazine she'd been reading when Kara stepped inside. "Kara, dear, you're back earlier than I expected…. Where's Sam?"

"He, um, went back to the restaurant." After seeing her to the door just as he'd promised. Out in the hallway, his gaze had searched hers, looking for some sign from her. But when all she did was remind him that the sheriff was waiting, he wished her a good-night and left….

"Are you all right, Kara?" Hope asked as she placed a comforting hand on her arm.

Taking a deep breath to calm her still-shaking nerves, she nodded. "I'm fine. Thank you for watching Timmy. How was he?"

"He's a sweet boy. Adorable, too, with those blond curls and green eyes. Takes after his father, doesn't he?"

Heart lodged in her throat, Kara stared at the other woman. "He—what?"

Hope peered from behind the frames of her glasses. "I was asking if he takes after his father."

It's a simple question, Kara. Hardly complicated. It doesn't mean she knows...she can't *know.*

"Yes, I suppose he does."

Kara wished the older woman good-night and went to check on her nephew. A narrow slice of light illuminated the bed. Timmy was sleeping soundly with his dinosaur under one arm. She gave a sigh of relief seeing the sheets still tucked around him, a sign that nightmares hadn't plagued his dreams.

After getting ready for bed, Kara reached up to turn off the bathroom light. Her hand paused over the switch as she caught sight of her reflection. Somehow, she'd managed to brush her teeth, take off her makeup and smooth on her moisturizer all without looking herself in the eye, but now she couldn't seem to look away.

She should focus on the dark circles, proof of too many nights spent tossing and turning, but she stared at her lips instead. Her mouth certainly didn't look branded by Sam Pirelli's kiss. Oh, but that was how it felt.

This was a man who could take everything from her. She'd already lost Marti; Kara didn't know how she would survive losing Timmy, too. Yet somehow that risk, that horrible, heartbreaking choice she had to make—somehow that wasn't bad enough.

If she stayed, she could be in serious danger of losing her heart, as well.

It was a crazy thought after only knowing the man for two days, but when Sam kissed her, when he held her in his arms, her heart felt lighter than it had in years. With her arms wrapped around his broad shoulders, the weight of the secret she carried disappeared.

Right now, though, that secret pressed heavier than ever.

Meeting her gaze in the mirror, Kara felt as if she could see her sister's blue eyes, filled with disappointment, staring back at her.

You should have told him.

Like most businesses in Clearville, Sam's garage was closed on Sunday, but that didn't mean he took the day off. He liked having those hours to focus on the cars without fielding phone calls and walk-in clients.

But today, not even the peace and quiet was helping him pay attention to the engine in front of him. A slam of the side door alerted Sam to Will's arrival and to the news that the kid was in an equally bad mood.

Tension filled the teen's skinny body as he stalked over to the car and slapped his hands down on the side of the open hood. "I told you I could take of myself. I can handle Darrell."

Straightening away from the sedan's engine, Sam wiped his hands on a nearby rag. "I was only trying to help."

"Help. You know where my mom is right now? She's picked up a double shift at the diner today so she'll have the money to go bail that jerk's sorry ass out of jail tomorrow! How does that help?"

Sam wanted to point out the fight hadn't been his fault—which was the only reason *his* sorry ass wasn't sitting in jail right then, too. But he figured that wasn't something Will wanted to hear.

The teen glared at him from across the sedan's raised hood. "I'm not some kid you need to look out for. I'm old enough to take of myself and my mom."

As Will stormed out of the garage, Sam let the boy go. He needed time to cool off. Time that Sam had decided to give Kara, as well. He still wanted that second chance, but first there was someone else he wanted to see.

The ringing bell over the Hope Chest door announced his arrival before he set foot inside. Normally, the antiques shop wouldn't be open, but over dinner Sophia had mentioned they'd received a large delivery of new-old items that she and Hope needed to arrange. He squeezed between the crowded shelves as he followed the sound of female voices to the back of the store.

Both his sister and Hope frowned as they caught sight of him, and for the first time in a long time, he didn't have a smart-ass comeback to deflect the disappointment and concern in their gazes.

Man, the Clearville grapevine was alive and buzzing if word of the fight had already reached them.

"Sam..." Sophia exchanged an unreadable glance with her mentor. "We didn't expect you to stop by."

"Yeah, well, I wanted to thank Hope for babysitting last night. I appreciate it."

Hope cleared her throat. "Timmy's a sweet boy."

"Yeah, he's a cute kid. I don't suppose he gave you much trouble."

"Oh, just the usual—seeing what he could get away with, with the babysitter. Multiple drinks of water, pleas for a snack, then a few trips to the bathroom."

Sam smiled. He'd always hated bedtime as a kid. "That sounds familiar."

"Does it now?" Hope murmured with another look at Sophia, this one weighted with enough unspoken urgency to grab hold of Sam's attention and not let go.

"Okay, what's going on with the knowing looks between the two of you?"

His sister twisted at the silver ring she wore, a dead give-away to her nervousness. "You remember the slideshow Jake and I had at our wedding? The pictures of us as kids and growing up? Hope helped me and Mom go through all our albums to pick out those pictures and decide which music worked best and—"

"Sophia, dear."

Shooting her friend a flustered look, his sister took a deep breath. "Right. Anyway, in looking through the al-bums, Hope saw a lot of pictures of you, too, Sam. Pictures of you when you were a little a boy. Pictures of you when you were...Timmy's age."

His sister let those words dangle and Sam waited for something more to come of the conversation. Something that might actually make sense. "And?" he prompted when the two women continued to look at him in anticipation.

Finally Hope stepped forward, pinning him with a knowing look. "And that boy, Sam Pirelli, is carbon copy of you when you were little."

Sam narrowed his gaze at the older woman, not liking the direction this conversation was going. "What are you saying, Hope?"

"I'm not saying anything. I'm asking." She took a deep breath. "Is Timmy...could Timmy be your son?"

"What?" The word exploded out of him with the force of disbelief and anger. "No! Do you really think I've had a kid all these years and didn't bother to tell anyone? Is that the kind of man—the kind of father—you think I am?"

"Take it easy, Sam! I know you wouldn't hide something like that," Sophia reassured him. "But Kara is Timmy's aunt, right? So what do you know about his mother?"

Nothing. He knew next to nothing about Kara's sister. Which was only slightly less than he knew about Kara. The evasive answers, her silence when it came to talking about herself…

"Kara said he'd just turned four. Can you think back?" Sophia asked softly. "Around five years ago…"

Five years? He couldn't think back to the past five minutes. He felt like he'd been dropped into the middle of a nightmare with no way of knowing how he got there and no idea how to get out.

"This is crazy. You're comparing twenty-five-year-old snapshots of me to a kid who has blond hair and making the leap that he's my son? No way."

"Why don't you take me to meet him, Sam?" Sophia pressed. "I've looked at those same pictures Hope was talking about my whole life. I know better than she does what you looked like as a kid. We can stop by and invite Kara and Timmy to breakfast. If you're right and there's nothing to Hope's idea, then no harm done."

Say no. Tell her no. The words raced through his brain like race cars on a track, looping over and over again. If he said yes, if he entertained just for a moment that Hope might be right…his life would change. He could feel it in his bones, the pressure building inside, urging him to run now.

But he couldn't run from this. Not if he ever wanted to look himself—to look his family—in the eye again.

"All right. Let's go."

The ride to the hotel took only minutes with Sophia sitting silently in the passenger seat beside him, but the car that he'd promised Timmy was fast enough to outrun monsters seemed to crawl through the town's deserted, early-morning streets.

Everything still looked the same—the Victorian shops, the profusion of colorful flower boxes, the wrought-iron benches and old-fashioned light posts. But Sam already had the feeling his entire world had changed.

As he pulled into the hotel's circular drive, he heard Sophia's gasp and followed her gaze. Not to the front of the building but to the parking lot where Kara and Timmy were walking toward her minivan. "Sam."

Sophia reached out and gripped his arm. She didn't say anything other than his name, but it was enough to tell him what she saw. What he'd refused to see.

Timmy was his son, and Kara had been lying to him from the moment they met.

Chapter Six

"Going somewhere?"

Kara stilled with her hand on the driver's side door of the minivan, frozen by the chill in the masculine voice behind her. Sam's voice.

He knows.

For a split second, she imagined diving into the seat, starting the engine and peeling out like a getaway driver in a movie. Motor racing, wheels screaming, she'd escape with Timmy in a cloud of dust. It was a crazy thought, and deep down, Kara knew she wasn't going anywhere. "Sam..."

She turned to face him only to wish she hadn't. The light in his eyes, his teasing smile, the spark of attraction simmering beneath the surface, all of it was gone. Regret slammed into her. She'd had the chance to tell him last night. She'd had any number of chances to tell him, but she'd been too afraid. And now, now her worst nightmare was coming true.

"Tell me the truth," he demanded. "Is Timmy mine? Is he my..." He seemed to stumble over the word. "Is he my son?"

Despite the shock of Sam discovering the truth, the quiet intensity of his voice got to Kara. The way he'd spoken the words softly enough so Timmy, sitting in the booster seat in the back, couldn't overhear. Putting the little boy's well-being above his own feelings.

Because that's what a parent did.

Silently, she nodded.

"Why didn't you tell me?" The muscles in his jaw hardened to granite as he forced the next words out. "*Were* you going to tell me?"

The guilt for keeping silent, for thinking even briefly about staying silent, must have shown on her face, giving Sam the only answer he needed.

Turning his back on her, he slid open the back door to the van, and Kara's heart stopped in her chest. "What... what are you doing?" Was that it? One question about Timmy's paternity and now Sam was going to take him away from her? "You can't—"

"Hey, Timmy."

Kara's protest faded away as Sam addressed his son. Wonder filled his voice, and Kara could almost imagine another lifetime where Sam would have spoken those same words as he held his infant son for the first time. But Marti had stolen that from him along with all the moments since—Timmy's first smile, first tooth. His wide, drooling grin as he gleefully learned to crawl, his far more cautious steps as he learned to walk. Fate had robbed Sam of those precious moments with his son.

Just as, years earlier, it had robbed her of a lifetime with her daughter.

How could she have considered doing the same thing to Sam? "Sam, I am so sorry."

The whispered words barely made it past the lump in her throat, and if he heard them, he gave no indication. "Did you have breakfast yet this morning?" he was asking the little boy who shook his head.

"Nuh-uh. Aunt Kara said we could go to the diner."

"Yeah, well, how about this? That's my sister, Sophia, over there. She works with Miss Hope, the nice lady who took care of you last night. What do you think about going to the diner and having breakfast with them?"

Beyond the width of Sam's shoulders, Kara could see the uncertainty written in her nephew's face. "Sam."

Ignoring her half-formed protest, he held out his hand to the little boy. Timmy hesitated, and as reluctant as she was to let him go, the anticipation tightening Sam's body nearly broke her heart. She could feel him bracing for a rejection, and she had to stop herself from laying a comforting hand on his broad shoulder. But what could she say that wouldn't turn him against her?

Give him time? He doesn't know you?

Those platitudes would only point to the time Sam missed and the son he didn't know.

But Timmy surprised her by scrambling across the backseat and sliding his dimpled hand into Sam's wide, callused palm. "You and Aunt Kara have to come, too," he declared as he reached for her hand, as well.

Her gaze met Sam's. For a brief moment, the image of Timmy caught in a tug-of-war between them flashed through her mind. She couldn't let that happen. *They* couldn't let that happen.

"That sounds great, buddy. Your Aunt Kara and I will meet you at the diner in a few minutes, okay?"

Timmy gave a sigh but rallied quickly. "Can I get waffles?"

"You bet," Sam agreed, and Kara knew he would have promised the boy the moon.

"With strawberries?"

"Strawberries *and* whipped cream."

The little boy beamed up at Sam. A sweet tooth was something they had in common, Kara thought as she remembered the piece of pie Sam had brought to her hotel room. The kindness he'd shown. "Sam…"

He turned his back on her as he led Timmy over to Sophia. Watching the two of them walk away—man and boy, father and son—Kara couldn't help feeling she'd let something so much sweeter than chocolate silk pie slip through her fingers.

"Don't worry." Sam's voice cut across Kara's raw nerves as she watched Sophia disappear down the street with Timmy. "My family's not going to keep him away from you."

The verbal slap stung. So did knowing that Sam wouldn't believe anything she said now that she'd lied to him. If she'd been up front, if she'd been honest…

Too late for that.

"Get in."

"What?" Too startled by the demand, she was still standing outside the minivan's open door by the time Sam circled the hood and climbed into the passenger seat. She'd assumed Sam had sent Timmy and his sister on to the diner so they could talk, but a ten second head start didn't give them much time. "Are we going to the diner?"

"Not yet."

"Then where?"

"I don't care. Just drive."

Kara wasn't surprised when Sam rolled the window down all the way, letting in a rush of air as she drove through the quiet streets. She sensed he needed the feeling of freedom right then.

"Who's Timmy's mother?"

"My sister was Marti Starling."

His breath escaped in a deep exhale. Because the name offered further proof that Timmy really was his? Because he'd just realized Marti was dead? Kara didn't know, and Sam didn't offer any explanations.

"How did she die?"

"In a small plane crash." Kara's hands tightened on the wheel, but she actually found it easier to talk with her gaze focused on the road ahead rather than looking into Sam's eyes. She didn't know what she'd see—sorrow, sympathy—but it was easier not to face it. "She'd been dating someone," Kara blurted out. "I'm sorry. I feel like everything I'm saying is making this worse."

"I don't think you can make this worse," he ground out. "But I haven't seen your sister in five years. I'm sure she went out with any number of guys since then."

"So you weren't—"

"Weren't what? In love?" he asked. "I don't know what answer would make this situation better. That what we felt *was* love and yet she didn't bother to tell me I'd fathered a child? Or that what we had didn't mean anything—and yet, together we created a child?"

Kara didn't think there was a right or wrong answer. But she did want to know the truth. Had Sam been in love with her sister?

Almost as if reading her thoughts, he said, "I cared about Marti. We clicked when we met, and I thought maybe we had…something. But I was only in San Diego for a few weeks, and when the calls and emails stopped, I thought that was it. I never imagined she'd keep something like this from me." He gave a rough laugh as he pounded his fist against the padded door. "Guess keeping secrets is a Starling family trait, though, isn't it, Kara?"

"That's not fair—" The furious look he shot her backed the words into her throat.

"You really want to talk about what's not fair?"

Kara drew in a shaky breath that did little to calm her nerves. This wasn't a conversation she could have behind the wheel of a car. Passing a sign pointing visitors to a scenic spot, she pulled off the road and into a small turn-out overlooking the ocean. "If you'll give me a chance to explain—"

"Like the chance you gave me?"

After shoving the gear shift into Park, Kara climbed from the vehicle. An early morning haze blanketed the ocean view, but the water was calm, the waves a soothing wash against the beach. Too bad the peaceful view did nothing to ease the storm of emotion raging inside her.

Or the one inside Sam, she thought, wincing as the car door slammed shut behind her.

"So, let's hear it," he demanded as he joined her near the guardrail at the edge of the overlook. "Explain why you didn't tell me who you are. Who Timmy is. Explain why you played me."

Kara gasped. Did he really think she'd used some kind of feminine wiles against him? She could only imagine how he would have laughed if he knew how pathetic and few her encounters with the opposite sex were. "That's not what I was doing!"

"What else would you call it? You knew Timmy is my son. You knew I had no idea that I'm his father—"

"And I had no idea what kind of father you would be! I didn't know anything about you except that you slept with my sister five years ago. And I was just supposed to hand my nephew over to a complete stranger?"

"Yeah, I'm a complete stranger. But whose fault is that? And who the hell gave you the right to decide if I'm good enough to be his father?"

"My sister did when she died and named me Timmy's guardian!"

Her voice carried out over the water, and only then did Kara realize she was shouting and the dampness on her face wasn't from the moisture in the air. Wiping at her cheeks, she took a deep breath. "I needed to be sure—so sure," she stressed, "that you would be a good father."

Her struggle for calm seemed to take the edge off Sam's anger, but the bitterness was still loud and clear as he asked, "And one date decides that, huh, professor? You teachers love to spring pop quizzes on students, right? So you sat across from me at that table last night, checking off everything I did wrong, determining whether or not I'd be a failure as a father."

"That's not what I was doing! I just wanted to see what kind of man you are and to try and decide what's best for Timmy. If you can't believe anything else I say, at least believe that."

He sank back against the guardrail, his forearms pulled tight as he gripped the metal. "Where was Timmy? When Marti…"

"With me. The guy she'd been seeing had a pilot's license and his own plane. He wanted to take Marti down to Mexico. She asked me to watch him, and well, I rarely said no."

Another silence followed, finally broken by Sam's gruff voice. "Thank you."

"For what?"

"For saving my son."

Kara's startled gaze met his. "Saving him?"

"I might not have known your sister as well as I thought I did," Sam admitted, "but unless she changed a lot in the past five years, she wasn't the type to miss out on a trip to Mexico. Or, hell, a trip to anywhere. What would she have done if you hadn't been able to watch Timmy?"

Kara's faced paled at his words. "I try not to think about it," she confessed softly.

His own gut clenched when he thought of the close call and what might have happened if not for Kara. She'd kept Timmy safe, but she'd lost her only sibling. He couldn't imagine what she'd gone through. He fiercely loved his brothers and sister. As strong as his family was, that kind of tragedy would devastate the Pirellis.

"I'm sorry about Marti. It's hard to believe she's gone."

"Sometimes I still can't believe it. She left a letter for me. I have it with me if you'd like to read it."

At his nod, Kara went back to the minivan and pulled a folded piece of paper from her purse. Kara was watching closely as she handed him the letter, and Sam wished he had some privacy for this moment. Sucking in a deep breath, he opened the page and started to read.

Kara—

My big sis...I'm not sure which of us is more surprised right now—me to be writing a letter like this or you to be reading it. You know I've never been much on planning for the future, but I hope you've seen that having Timmy has changed me. At least a little.

You stood by me when I got pregnant, and you've been there for me and Timmy every step of the way since.

You've always encouraged me to talk about Timmy's father—to tell him about Timmy. I know you think it was wrong of me to keep his birth a secret all these years, and maybe you're right.

I know it's a lot to ask, but if anything did happen to me, I'd like you to take Timmy to meet his father, Sam Pirelli.

I know we haven't always seen eye to eye, but you've been the best big sister any little sister could ask for. I love you.

Marti

"She never told you anything about me?"

"No. My parents and I tried to get her to tell us, but she would never say who you were. When she died, I thought—"

"That you would raise him."

"Yes, that's what I thought. That's what I want."

Well, if he wanted honesty from Kara, she couldn't be much more up front than that. Determination lifted her chin and she met his gaze head-on, but he could see her vulnerability in the trembling lips she pressed tightly together. What was she trying to hide? Her own doubts and fears? Sam wasn't sure, but he knew it could only be a fraction of the emotions pummeling him from all sides.

"What do you want, Sam?" For a split second, the years were swept away and he was back in school, getting called out in front of the entire class as the teacher grilled him with questions they both knew damn well he didn't have the answers to. But his old defenses—a quick comeback and an easy smile—had deserted him. His thoughts were so tangled he didn't know where one idea began or the next ended, and he'd never felt less like smiling.

What did he want? Did Kara honest to God think he had some kind of backup plan for something like this? Or was she simply waiting, like his teachers had, for him to admit he didn't have a damn clue?

But this wasn't just about him. Nothing in life could be just about him anymore, because now there was Timmy. A cute, serious, smart little boy to think about. A little boy who'd already lost his mother and who Sam was well aware now looked to his aunt for comfort and security.

As hard as it was for Sam to wrap his mind around the idea that he had a son, the thought of Kara and Marti being sisters was almost as unbelievable. The woman he remembered from five years ago had been lively and outgoing, and on occasion more than a little outrageous. The time they'd spent together had been filled with late-night parties, bar hopping at the hottest clubs in San Diego. He couldn't picture Kara in any of those places.

Up until a few days ago, he would have told anyone who asked that Marti was exactly his type of woman. But if that was true, then why did he have such a hard time remembering exactly what she looked like? The sound of her voice? The scent of her perfume?

Why was the face of every woman he'd dated before such a blur? All he could see—all he could think about—was Kara. The subtle arch of her eyebrows, the slim shape of her nose, the high, elegant cheekbones. He felt like he'd made a study of the tempting lift to her lips that promised a full smile to the man lucky enough to earn one.

Her voice, murmuring his name in the split second before he'd kissed her, still echoed in his ears, and it was the whisper that had awakened him that very morning. He'd carried the faint hint of her perfume home on his clothes, the scent haunting his senses.

He couldn't explain the intensity of his attraction any more than he could deny it—or the way Kara had used that attraction against him. If he'd stopped to think about it, he should have known a woman like her—a college professor—would never go for a blue-collar guy like him. But then again, Sam supposed thinking had never been his strong suit.

The memory of the way she'd played him—the humiliation, the hurt—stoked Sam's anger again, but he pushed the emotion aside to deal with at another time. He had Timmy to think about now. And there was only one thing Sam was sure of in that moment.

"He's my son, and I want to get to know him."

Chapter Seven

"If you don't take a breath," Sam said with a glance from the driver's seat, "you're gonna pass out before we ever get to my parents' house."

"I'm breathing," Kara argued. Careful, controlled breaths to calm her nerves and keep her from throwing up on the floorboards. She was glad Sam had offered to drive. Her hands, tightly folded in her lap, wouldn't stop shaking, and she knew she'd be a mess behind the wheel.

Unclenching her fingers, she smoothed her damp palms over the skirt of her dress.

She'd taken longer than usual with her appearance. She'd pulled her hair back in a low ponytail tied by a red ribbon to match the trim beneath the bodice of her white, halter-style sundress. Another red band circled the full skirt just below her knee. Not that what she wore would change what Sam's family thought of her.

What Sam thought of her.

He had dressed more casually than the night before in faded jeans and a soft grey henley shirt. He'd combed his dark blond hair back, but the natural curl was already resisting. Kara couldn't imagine what it was about that that made him seem vulnerable. That made her want to reach out and not only smooth the curl back from his forehead, but soothe away the worried lines she saw there despite his reassurance that everything would be fine.

"Remember," he told her, "this is just dinner with friends."

He'd agreed, reluctantly, that telling Timmy Sam was his father now wasn't a good idea. The little boy was still trying to cope with the death of his mother. The sudden appearance of a father he'd never met would be too much. Instead, Kara had suggested the two of them get to know each other under the guise of Sam simply being a friend.

So far, Sam had played the part just right. After meeting them at the hotel, he had kept up an easy, one-sided monologue about the swing and huge backyard at his parents' house, about his niece, Maddie, who was looking forward to meeting Timmy, about his mother who made the best spaghetti ever. With meatballs, he reassured the little boy, because you can't have spaghetti without meatballs.

"I know, but what about your family? Are they willing to take things slowly?"

"It's not going to be easy." Glancing in the rear view mirror, Sam said, "They're going to want to welcome Timmy with open arms. Family means everything to them."

Kara didn't doubt that. Part of her even wished it wasn't true. Why did Sam have to come from such a close-knit family? It would be so much easier to convince Sam that Timmy's place was with her if he had dysfunctional relatives scattered throughout the country. So much easier to convince herself…

Wasn't the way Sam had described the Pirellis—loud, loving, always involved in each other's lives—exactly the kind of family Kara had longed for as a child? Her own parents had always been too consumed by their careers, too committed to the hospital to spend time at home. Kara had tried hard to gain their approval by following their rules—to study hard, to excel at school—yet her perfect grades were simply expected and rarely celebrated.

But that wasn't how she would raise Timmy. Yes, her nephew was smart, and she wanted to encourage him to make the most of his gifts, but she wouldn't weigh him down with her expectations the way her parents had when she was a child. The way they still did, Kara acknowledged, thinking of the nomination for department chair. She still wasn't sure the position was right for her, but would she be able to withstand their disappointment and disapproval if she turned it down?

Kara shoved the thought aside. She'd face that decision when the time came. For now, her focus was on Timmy and the future she pictured for the two of them. But as Sam pulled up in front of a sprawling ranch-style farmhouse with every window lit in welcome, she couldn't help wondering why a family of two suddenly seemed too small.

"Kara, this is my Mom, Vanessa, and my dad, Vince, and my oldest brother, Nick. This is Kara Starling and… her nephew, Timmy."

As they stepped inside his parents' house, Kara barely registered the living room's warm, comfortable furnishings, hardwood floors and cozy stone fireplace before she was surrounded by Sam's family.

His father, Vince, and older brother Nick were imposing men with dark hair and piercing eyes. She had a hard time reading their expressions as they saw Timmy for the first time, but Vanessa Pirelli's eyes immediately filled with tears as she gazed down at the little boy. "Timmy, it is so good to meet you."

She reached out, but Timmy shrank back, hiding behind Kara's full skirt.

His reaction only showed Kara that she and Sam were doing the right thing in taking these introductions slowly. "I'm sorry," she told Sam's mother as she placed a comforting hand on Timmy's narrow shoulder. "He's a little shy around new people…."

"Of course, I understand." Vanessa wrapped her arms around her waist, and Kara sensed the other woman's almost desperate longing to pull Timmy into her arms. She certainly related to that feeling. She'd wanted to cling to her nephew and not let go since she'd first read Marti's letter.

Almost against her will, her gaze slid to the man at her side. Other than that initial moment when Sam held his hand out to his son, he hadn't tried to touch Timmy. Because he was afraid of overwhelming the boy? Or because he was already overwhelmed himself? It was hard to imagine anything knocking a man of Sam's size to his knees, but finding out he was a father clearly had.

Sam finished the introductions with his brother's fiancée, Darcy Dawson, a stunning redhead with an easy, infectious smile and Nick's daughter, Maddie.

"Where are Sophia and Jake?" he asked.

"Sophia called. She says she's tired, so she and Jake are staying in."

"And what about Drew?"

"He had a walk-through with a homeowner that he couldn't reschedule." Turning to Kara, Vanessa explained, "Drew builds custom houses and his clients can be somewhat demanding, but he'll be here in time for dinner."

"You really didn't have to go to so much trouble. We could have done this another day."

"Oh, no! We've already missed—" Vanessa cut off her words as she pulled her gaze from Timmy and forced a determined smile. "Tonight is perfect."

She stepped forward, but instead of trying to coax Timmy out from behind Kara, the older woman held out a hand to her granddaughter. "Maddie, dear, why don't you show Timmy the toy box? Maybe he can find something to play with until dinner is ready."

A toy box sat in the corner of the room, identical to the one Sam had at his office, but the initial on the front declared this one was Nick's. Easing Timmy out from behind her, Kara encouraged, "Go take a look, Timmy."

Maddie swung her ponytail over one shoulder in a move that made her appear the older, wiser cousin. "My gramma kept all kinds of toys from when my dad and uncles were kids. You'll like 'em, they're, like, retro."

"Hear that, hon, you're retro," Darcy teased.

The eldest Pirelli sibling rolled his eyes. "So glad you and my daughter think so."

As the two kids knelt in front of the toy box, Vince said, "Why don't we all have a seat? Might as well be comfortable."

Though *comfortable* was the perfect word to describe the casual furnishings of the room, Kara couldn't imagine feeling more unsettled until Sam placed his hand on her waist. She hadn't really thought of the back of her dress as particularly low, but his thumb brushed the naked skin of her back and a shiver raced down her spine to her toes and then up to the base of her neck, leaving goose bumps covering every inch along the way.

"So, Kara, what do you do for a living?" Vince asked as he claimed the recliner and his wife perched on the wide armrest beside him. Nick and Darcy had already settled into armchairs near the fireplace, the cozy patterned seats close enough that the newly engaged couple could link hands. Which left the sofa for Kara and Sam, who sat far closer than she would have preferred.

She tried making a pretense of adjusting her skirt and moving an inch or two away, but his thick, denim-clad thigh had pinned the material beneath its weight. Unless she wanted to have a tug-of-war in front of Sam's family, she was going to have to stay put.

Plastering a smile on her face, she said, "I'm a teacher."

"College professor," Sam corrected. It should have sounded like he was bragging about her accomplishments, and yet somehow didn't.

"I teach literature at a private college."

"What do you think—"

Vince's question was cut off by raised voices coming from the corner. "That's my book, Timmy."

"But I want to read it."

"It's for big kids. There's no pictures."

"I want to read that one!" Timmy voice, little more than a whisper as he'd greeted his new relatives, now came through loud and clear.

"Timmy," Kara scolded, recognizing the stubborn tilt to his chin all too well. "It's not yours."

"Maddie, hon, why don't you go ahead and give him the book," Darcy suggested.

"But Darcy!" Exasperation filled Maddie's voice. "He can't even read it."

"I can too!" Opening the book, he started to read.

Maddie's jaw dropped almost comically. "Dad, Rachel's brother is way older than Timmy is, like six, and he can hardly read at all!" When he finished the first paragraph, she said, "Read the next part."

Timmy glanced over at Kara, and she gave a silent nod. He bent his head over the book and sounded out words that many six-year-olds wouldn't know. He stopped at the end of the page. "Told you I could read it."

"Timmy," Kara admonished.

"Well, he did tell her," Nick pointed out pragmatically.

Realizing everyone was staring, Timmy thrust the book back at Maddie and rushed into Kara's arms. For the first time since entering the Pirelli home, she took a deep breath as she cradled his body against hers.

It was only then that she realized the rest of the room had fallen completely silent. Glancing sideways at Sam, she murmured, "Like I said, he's really smart."

"That was incredible!" Vanessa gushed, shock still evident in her wide eyes. "To read at that level at his age..."

"We first realized how advanced Timmy is when he was around two, and he's been attending a preschool for gifted children since he turned three."

"I don't think Clearville has anything like that," Vanessa murmured, shooting a worried glance at her husband.

Kara knew the town didn't. She'd already checked—another point in favor of Timmy returning to San Diego with her. Pressing a kiss onto the top of his head, she tightened her arms around his small form.

Sitting on the picnic table in the backyard, Sam exhaled deeply. He'd never before felt the need to escape from his own family, from the house where he'd grown up, but he couldn't have stayed inside one more minute. The old farmhouse was good-sized and had comfortably fit the Pirelli family and all four kids when they were growing up. But sitting in the kitchen tonight, he'd felt the walls closing in around him and the desperate, overwhelming urge to run.

Not that he'd gone far. The sound of voices drifted across

the freshly cut grass, and he doubted his reprieve would last for more than a minute or two. He'd take what he could and hope those few minutes would be enough for him to get his head on straight.

A son. He had a son. And he was *smart.*

Kara had told him, he'd give her that. At first, he'd only thought she was being a proud aunt and then later, he'd been too angry to listen as she explained all the reasons why his son would be better off with her. But the longer he sat in the living room with Kara answering all of his mother's questions, the greater the weight of her gaze pressed on him.

He's smart, Sam. Really smart.

The slap of the screen door closing interrupted his thoughts, and Sam glanced back over his shoulder. In the faint light from the back porch, he saw his brothers heading his way. At least they'd brought beer, he thought, seeing the bottles in their hands.

"Thanks," he said as Drew handed him the cold drink before leaning against the edge of the table to take a long drink of his own. Nick claimed a spot on the bench beside Sam, sitting backward to face the house.

For a few minutes, no one spoke, the wind in the trees and faint clatter from the open kitchen window were the only sounds. Finally Nick commented wryly, "I really thought my engagement would be the biggest news to hit this family for a long time to come, but that sure didn't last."

Drew snorted softly. "You know our baby brother likes all the attention for himself."

"Baby brother's sitting right here and he's big enough to whip your ass." Sam's bravado faded away as he remembered Kara's reaction to the fight with Darrell. Didn't seem like he'd be getting in any friendly fights with his brothers soon, not if he wanted to change Kara's image of him.

"You need a lawyer."

"What?"

Nick glanced to the side to meet his startled gaze. "You know how much I hate them, but you need to talk to a lawyer. The sooner, the better. That boy's a Pirelli, and he deserves your name."

He flinched. With Marti having kept his identity a secret, obviously Timmy carried her last name. Which meant the father was listed as unknown on his birth certificate. Sam's hand tightened around the beer bottle, the truth of that realization cutting deep. He hadn't known about Timmy, Timmy still didn't know about him, and it would take a hell of a lot more than changing a piece of paper to fix that.

Still, he told Nick, "I'll get in touch with a lawyer."

Nick pushed away from the bench and then reached out to tap his bottle against Sam's. "Congratulations, by the way."

"Yeah, it's a boy," Sam answered with a rough laugh.

As Nick walked back toward the house, Sam took another deep breath and looked over at Drew. His brother hadn't seconded Nick's advice, which meant he had his own ideas about what Sam should do. Ideas he'd likely play over in his head before ever saying them out loud.

Drew would speak his mind in his own time, and prodding him wouldn't make him spill the beans any faster. Used to bug the heck out of him when they were kids. Sam drummed his fingers against the cool side of the glass bottle. Kids, nothing! It bugged the crap out of him now.

"Nick has a point about seeing the lawyer," Drew said finally. "Timmy needs to have the Pirelli name, and you need to look into setting up life insurance and writing a will."

Life insurance. Wills. Part of Sam wanted to laugh at the thought. Those things were for old people, right? But where would he be if Marti had thought that way? He knew exactly where. He'd still be driving down the highway in the 'Vette, wind in his hair, as he took a few hairpin turns rushing toward his dreams. He'd be the man he'd been until Kara showed up and everything changed.

"You're right," he sighed. "I have to think about Timmy now."

"And about Kara?"

He frowned. "What do you mean?"

"I saw the way Kara looks at Timmy. She wants to raise him."

"I know," Sam said, scraping his thumbnail against the slightly soggy label on the beer bottle. "She told me."

His brother's eyebrows rose slightly at that as he eased away from the table to sit at Sam's side. "Well, that's honest."

Ever since he'd confronted Kara, she'd been completely truthful. Maybe more truthful than he would have liked. Knowing she wanted to raise Timmy was forcing Sam to make a decision he didn't know if he could make.

This was too important to screw up, and what if he failed? What if he couldn't be the father Timmy needed? Sam took a swallow of beer, but the drink did little to ease the gnawing at his gut.

Kara had been a part of his son's life since the day he was born. She'd loved him during all the years when Sam had been completely absent from Timmy's life.

That wasn't his fault, and Marti should have told him the truth, but none of that mattered because it didn't change reality.

Sam was a total stranger. Throw into an already complicated equation that Kara was kind and caring and *smart* and even Sam could see how those pluses added up to a woman who was the perfect person to raise his son.

"She loves him," Sam told him brother.

"I can see that," Drew agreed. "But I saw something else. When she wasn't looking at Timmy, she was looking at you."

He'd felt the weight of Kara's stare more than once throughout the evening, almost as if she was willing him to see reason and let Timmy go back home with her. Or worse, that she was looking into his mind and seeing how torn he was between grabbing hold of his son and not letting go, and wanting to run for the hills and never look back.

What kind of a father felt that way? Not his, that was for sure. And not Nick. His older brother had raised Maddie as a single parent since she was three years old.

"So what's going on between the two of you?" his brother asked.

"I don't know what you mean."

"Come on, Sam. I know you better than that. You're the ladies' man, the lover of women." Drew raised his eyebrows along with his beer. "You have to know when one is interested in you."

"This is different."

"Different because of Timmy? Or different because of Kara?"

Sam had thought Kara was interested. That initial spark when they'd met, the night they'd spent talking in her hotel room, the kisses they'd shared… But that was all before he'd realized the secret she'd been keeping from him. She had promised to tell him the truth, but even if he could trust what she said, Sam knew when it came to Kara, he could no longer trust what he felt.

"Carefully, Timmy," Kara warned as her nephew reached for the last of the empty dinner plates on the table. "You don't want to drop anything."

Vanessa glanced back over her shoulder with a rich laugh, up to her elbows in soapy dishwater. "You've met my sons. Anything that survived those three is built to last. Honestly, I think they broke fewer dishes when they were Timmy's age. At least back then, they made an attempt to be careful."

Maybe that was why the older woman had shooed the men from the kitchen as soon as dinner was over. Darcy and Maddie were cutting pieces of the cake they'd brought, purchased from the local baker who, according to Sam's niece, made the best desserts ever, while Kara and Timmy "helped" with the dishes.

"Good job, sweetheart. What a big help you are," Vanessa said as he handed her the plate.

Not to be outdone, Maddie called out over her shoulder. "I'm helping, too, Gramma."

"Yes, I see that, Maddie," Vanessa said, the twinkle in her eye revealing she was well aware her granddaughter was mostly helping herself to an extra finger or two full of frosting.

Timmy beamed shyly up at Vanessa. "I like helping. I never get to help at Grandmother and Grandfather's house. That's Mrs. Waymer's job."

Kara felt her face heat at her nephew's innocent, yet telling statement and Vanessa's questioning glance. "Mrs. Waymer is my parents' housekeeper," she explained.

The woman had worked for her parents for almost as long as Kara could remember. The quiet, gray-haired woman was good at her job, keeping every inch of the Starling house spotless. She took extra pride in making their kitchen, with its state-of-the-art, stainless-steel appliances, white marble countertops and black granite floors shine. That décor, like everything else, was a world away from the Pirelli kitchen.

Here, rich, earth tones warmed the space, from the oak cabinets and matching table and chairs to the green-checked cushions and napkins, to the vibrant red pots and pans. The stove and refrigerator could almost qualify as antiques, but like the butcher block counter, they'd been well cared for and wore their age with pride. Lace curtains hung from the windows, and a rooster-shaped clock counted out the many happy hours the Pirellis shared during family dinners.

Kara couldn't remember her parents' kitchen ever being so filled with people or with so much laughter…or love. The emotion permeated the air the same way the scent of tomatoes, onions and garlic bubbling away on the stove had.

"A housekeeper," Vanessa echoed. "I see."

Kara shifted beneath the older woman's speculative gaze as she reached for a glass in the dish drain and started to dry. She had a feeling that kitchen cleanup might not have been the only reason Vanessa had asked her to stay behind. "My parents are both surgeons. Their careers keep them very busy."

"This must be so hard on them." Vanessa said quietly as Timmy skipped back over to the table to collect the silverware. "I can't even imagine. To lose a child…"

Kara's hands stilled on the damp cotton. The small locket she wore pressed heavily against her heart, but she forced herself to wipe the gingham towel over the smooth glass.

"And for you and Timmy, as well. The poor boy."

"I want to thank you for understanding why I—why Sam and I want to take things slowly. I know this has been a surprise for all of you, too. Just showing up the way we did."

"Children—grandchildren especially," Vanessa added with a wink, "are always a blessing."

Kara reached for another glass, but as her hands continued the monotonous chore of drying dishes, her thoughts drifted back in time. How Vanessa Pirelli's view differed from her own parents! They'd been furious twelve years ago when Kara finally found the courage to confess she was pregnant.

The only saving grace was that she'd called from school. She hadn't had to see the disappointment and anger in her father's face. But, more than a decade later, she could still hear it in his voice.

How could you be so foolish! To ruin your life by making such a stupid mistake!

"And Timmy is more of a blessing than most children."

Thinking the older woman was referring to the time she'd missed, the grandchild she almost hadn't had the opportunity to know, Kara blurted out, "I'm sorry that my sister kept him from you all these years."

"Kara, it's all right," Vanessa interrupted. "You have nothing to apologize for. Your sister, she loved Timmy, didn't she?"

"Yes." Kara might not have understood why her sister had kept her silence or what had prompted her to leave the letter behind, but that one thing she trusted without a doubt. "She loved him."

"And she must have thought she was doing what was best for her child. That's all any mother can do."

Doing what was best for her child. It couldn't have been easy to be gracious toward a woman who'd kept their grandchild a secret, yet Kara read a true sympathy in Vanessa's eyes.

"But that isn't what I was meant when I called Timmy a special blessing." She smiled at her newfound grandson, who still held a handful of dirty silverware but was distracted by the pieces of chocolate cake Darcy and Maddie were setting out on the sideboard. “I think that boy is exactly what Sam needs.”

“Needs?”

“Sam has always been so focused. His father would call it pigheaded, but since I’ve always figured Sam got it from him, who am I to argue?” Vanessa gave a light laugh. “From the time Sam was not much older than Timmy, he could name every make and model of car on the road. Some kids are born with a silver spoon. My youngest son might as well have come out holding a socket wrench.”

“Well, that’s good, isn’t it? To have a calling?” Kara had always wanted to be a teacher, but not a college professor. She’d dreamed of teaching kindergarten until the reality of being around children became too painful.

If she were named department chair, she couldn’t help wondering if her dream wouldn’t be slipping even further from her fingers. She’d have to give up some of her classes to take on the administrative duties of overseeing her fellow teachers. The promotion was supposed to be a step up, but she couldn’t help wonder if she’d be moving in the wrong direction.

“Yes and no,” Vanessa sighed. “I’ve always felt Sam was so focused on that one path, that he’s never bothered to look around, to explore other options. I think Timmy will be just the incentive Sam needs to open his eyes and see there’s more to life than being a good—or even a great—mechanic.”

“Things like being a good father,” Kara surmised.

The older woman made a soft sound of agreement before mildly adding, “And a good husband.”

“Oh!” A startled gasp escaped Kara as the glass she’d been drying nearly slipped from her fingers. “I’m so sorry. I’m not normally so clumsy.”

"No harm done," Vanessa assured her as she took the glass from her hands and placed it in the cupboard.

"And to think, I was worried about Timmy," Kara said with a forced laugh.

And now, thanks to one harmless comment, she had a whole new set of worries about a future she hadn't imagined. Worries about some nameless, faceless woman Sam might meet, a woman he would marry, a woman he would love…a woman who Timmy would someday call Mom.

Sam knew he couldn't hide out in the yard forever, but as he made his way back to the house and saw his father waiting on the front porch, he wished he'd stay away a little longer.

His foot barely hit the first step when Vince said, "I thought we raised you better than this, Sam."

He flinched at the gruff words, feeling like a kid again. Like a failure again. The sick kick in the gut was as familiar as it was hated, and Sam wanted to lash out the way he had before he'd learned to hide his true feelings behind a joke and a smile.

But there could be no joking about this.

"You did," Sam said as he joined his father at the railing. "You taught me family means everything and nothing is more important."

"And to respect women."

"Yes."

"Which means not walking away and leaving a girl pregnant."

Getting a girl pregnant meant getting married. It might have been old-fashioned, but as far as the Pirellis were concerned, it was the right thing to do. But would it have been the right thing for him and Marti? If she had come to him when she was pregnant, if he had done what his family expected and proposed, Sam couldn't imagine their marriage would have been anything other than wrong. But that argument would only further disappoint Vince, if that was even possible. "I'm sorry about how this happened."

"You have a lot of ground to cover, Sam. Four years of fatherhood to make up for in that boy's life, if you ever expect him to call you Dad."

The screen door slammed shut on his father's final words. *Dad.* Sam gripped the porch railing. He'd never given much thought to being a father. Oh, sure, maybe someday when he was older. When he was ready. But now…

"Ready or not," he muttered beneath his breath.

A creak on the porch alerted him to a soft step off to the right, and he tensed as Kara appeared out of the shadows. Great. "How much of that did you hear?"

"Enough," she admitted. "Your dad was pretty hard on you."

"He has reason to be."

"This isn't your fault, Sam. If Marti had told you—"

"But she didn't. And that is my fault. A woman that I was with didn't trust me enough to tell me I was going to be a father. What does that say about what she thought of me?"

He already knew the answer. Good enough for a good time, but not good enough to know about the child they created.

"Sam." Kara curved her palm over the arm he'd braced against the porch railing. The warmth and softness of her touch seeped into his skin. Into muscle, into bone. But he'd learned his lesson. He already knew Kara could reach deep enough inside him to pull out his heart.

"Not again," he ground out as he took an almost stumbling step back. He'd been fool enough to let Kara use his attraction against him once. It was a mistake he wasn't going to make again.

Chapter Eight

"Timmy, what are you doing?" Kara asked even though she could see for herself that her nephew was picking the golden raisins out of the muffin she'd bought him at Bonnie's Bakery.

The chocolate cake Nick had brought for dessert at the Pirellis' the night before had been as rich and decadent as promised, and Kara had decided to stop at the bakery for breakfast. She'd ordered muffins for both of them along with an herbal tea for herself and orange juice for Timmy. The bakery had two white wrought-iron bistro tables set up out front, and the weather—blue skies with only a hint of a breeze–was perfect for alfresco dining. The location was even better for four-year-old dining, considering the mess Timmy was making.

"I don't like raisins," he answered as he added another reject to the pile on his napkin. "They look like bugs."

"But you like bugs," she teased.

Timmy merely shot her a sly look from beneath the blond curls falling across his forehead and went back to dissecting his muffin.

It was such a simple and silly moment, and yet the rush of love she felt nearly overwhelmed her. Reaching up, she fingered the locket she wore around her neck. Even though she'd only been eighteen when she got pregnant, Kara never thought she would have another chance to be a mother. The risk of getting pregnant and losing another child…she wouldn't survive the loss. She'd buried that dream when she buried her daughter. But with Marti's death…

Kara would have given anything to bring her sister back, but it wasn't possible. What was possible was being a mother to Timmy. She would do all she could to keep Marti's spirit alive for the little boy, but he was only four. In time, his memories would start to fade, and Kara wanted to be there in her sister's place. *She* needed to be there, not some unknown woman Sam might find once fatherhood opened his eyes to the possibility of settling down.

Her mind rejected the very thought of some other woman raising Timmy. Of some other woman marrying Sam.

Kara sucked in a quick breath, stunned by the jealousy that rose up inside her, and immediately started choking. A bite of the rich, crumbly muffin caught in her throat, and only after a coughing fit and huge swallow of tea was she able to breathe again.

She wasn't jealous over Sam. She couldn't be jealous over Sam.

Eying her with a mixture of concern and curiosity, Timmy asked, "Was it a raisin? I told you they taste like bugs."

Wiping at her watering eyes, Kara said, "You told me they *look* like bugs."

"Aunt Kara ate a bug, Aunt Kara ate a bug."

She opened her mouth to argue, but she figured pointing out that raisins were actually dried-out grapes wouldn't do much for her cause. "Finish your muffin, Timmy."

A loud squeal of tires shattered the peaceful morning, and Kara glanced down the street with a frown. The shops on either side of the narrow road were already open, including the Hope Chest and the Beauty Mark, Darcy's boutique. Tourists and townspeople alike walked along the sidewalks and backed in and out of the few parking spaces. Hers wasn't the only head that turned at the out of place sound.

What kind of idiot would speed down Main Street?

She'd barely caught sight of the primer-spotted red Corvette when Timmy announced, "Hey, look, it's Sam!" The little boy turned around to kneel on the seat. He braced his small hands on the rounded back of the chair as the tires screeched to a halt in front of the bakery. "Wow, his car really is fast."

Fast and reckless. What was Sam thinking racing through the small streets and slamming on his brakes the way he had? But as soon as he climbed out and she saw his expression, Kara's irritation disappeared, immediately replaced by concern.

Telling Timmy to wait in his chair, she hurried out across the sidewalk and met Sam at the front of his car. "Sam, what's wrong?"

"What's wrong?" The panic she'd first seen on his face was quickly turning to anger as he stared at her like she'd been the one tearing down the road like a maniac. He ran his hands through his already tousled hair and closed his eyes as if trying to get a grip on his emotions.

Finally he opened his eyes and his arms dropped to his sides. "I went to the hotel this morning, but you weren't there. I checked the parking lot and the minivan was gone..."

And he thought she'd taken off. The words he didn't say were as clear as the ticking of the Corvette's engine. As clear as the fear lingering in his green eyes.

Sam cared about Timmy. This wasn't only about duty or responsibility or stepping up to the plate because it was what his family thought he should do. He cared about his son."

The realization split Kara's emotions in two. Part of her wished Sam was more like Curtis Graham, her college boyfriend—a man who could walk away from duty and responsibility without a second glance. But the other side of her was glad. She'd long believed that Timmy needed the right kind of male role model in his life. That a boy needed his dad.

"Sam..." A rush of empathy filled her, and she barely stopped herself from reaching out to reassure him.

Not again.

Her cheeks heated as she remembered his rejection on the porch the night before. The confusion and doubt on his handsome face had so perfectly mirrored her own, her heart had gone out to him and, without thought, her hands had followed...and she'd ended up making yet another mistake with the opposite sex.

Maybe, Kara thought as she knotted her fingers in front of her to keep them where they belonged, maybe she'd finally learned her lesson.

"I thought Timmy and I could look around the shops this morning," she explained, her voice as calm and gentle as when she spoke to her nephew. "I wasn't planning to buy anything, but I wanted the van here just in case, so I wouldn't have to worry about carrying packages back to the hotel."

Meeting his gaze head-on, she added, "I'm not going to leave, Sam." When she could still see the doubt in his expression, she reached inside the pocket of her beige slacks for the hotel key card. "Go back to the room if you want. All our clothes are still there."

Sam lifted a hand but instead of taking the key, he wrapped his fingers around hers. A frisson of electricity streaked up her arm, sending goose bumps rising in its wake, and Kara had to fight not to pull her arm away. "No," he said. "I trust you. I just freaked out for a minute."

That was something of an understatement, Sam admitted to himself. When he had knocked on the hotel-room door that morning and Kara hadn't answered, he'd started to worry. Kara had been quiet on the ride home from his parents' house, just as she'd been after their disaster of a date, and her words from that night had sounded like alarm bells through his head.

I won't be in town for long.

What was to stop Kara from leaving Clearville as unexpectedly as she'd arrived? After the search of the parking lot for her minivan came up empty, the need to find her overrode common sense. Spotting the two of them sitting outside the bakery, his first instinct had been to pull Timmy into his arms and never let him go. His second instinct? To grab hold of Kara....

It was a crazy thought, but he had to shove his hands in his back pockets to keep from burying his hands in her blond hair and kissing her until he could convince—himself? Convince her?—that the attraction between them was real.

Pushing the thought aside, he said, "I'm sorry I overreacted."

Her expression softened slightly at his gruff words, the same way it had when she'd reassured him she wouldn't leave town. But the walls had come back up so quickly, and

Sam didn't know what it would take to tear them down. He had to find some way to make her trust him. Hell, *he* had to find some way to trust *her,* or Timmy would always be caught between the two of them.

"It's all right," she said finally. She waved to the small table. "Why don't you join us for breakfast?"

Sam looked over to find Timmy watching closely, but the moment he made eye contact, the boy spun back around in his chair. "Hey, Timmy. How's it going?"

He mumbled something beneath his breath as he went back to picking at his—was that a *bran* muffin? Whatever it was, it wasn't the breakfast Sam remembered from his childhood. Most of his memories of early mornings started with bounding out of bed, rushing into Nick and Drew's room, eager to drag them out for a breakfast of sugary cereal eaten in front of early-morning cartoons. But only if they were up before their parents. On days when he slept in, he would wake to the scent of pancakes or eggs and bacon, and the sound of his parents laughing over their morning coffee.

He couldn't offer Timmy any of that.

Sam didn't know what it was he *could* offer Timmy besides the Pirelli name—something he'd lived without the past four years.

"We can't hear you, Timmy," Kara said as she sat back down in her chair. "Can you talk louder?"

"Hi, Sam."

The words weren't much more than a whisper, but Sam heard them loud and clear.

You have four years of fatherhood to make up for in that boy's life if you ever expect him to call you "Dad."

His father's words echoed in his thoughts. He couldn't cram four years into a few days, but he asked, "What do you think about the two of us hanging out and having some fun, Timmy?"

"Aunt Kara, too?"

"Yeah, sure. Aunt Kara's gonna have fun, too." Sam glanced over at the cool blonde, his eyebrows raised. The only way Timmy would relax would be if Kara let down her guard. And if he couldn't go over those walls, Sam thought, then maybe he'd be better off trying to get under her skin. "Right, Aunt Kara?"

"Yeah, sure," she mimicked with just enough sass to let him know she was up to the challenge.

Ready to have fun, Aunt Kara?

Those words, along with Sam's I-dare-you green eyes and devilish grin, had greeted her every morning for the past five days. And after a week of his teasing, his laughing, his *flirting,* a part of Kara wanted some serious revenge. She wanted to do something, anything, to knock that cocky smile off his face and show him that she wasn't the stuffy professor his laughing eyes accused her of being. She wasn't some boring old stick in the—

Kara caught her breath on a gasp as her sandal sank into the wet, sucking sand.

"Good job, Tim!" Sam called out from further down the beach. Father and son were ten yards or so from the rushing surf, playing catch with a small rubber football. Or rather Sam was playing "throw," while the little boy didn't want any part of catching the ball. Timmy was content to duck out of the way and wait for the ball to bounce to a stop before trying to toss it back.

Assuming he didn't get distracted by a small crab crawling along the edge of the surf or some smelly piece of seaweed washed up on shore.

"Okay, now throw it back, Timmy!" Sam called out as the ball landed at his son's feet.

Kara had to give Sam credit. He seemed determined to form a relationship with Timmy, but it was obvious to her he was going about it in all the wrong ways.

And you're not helping.

Marti's voice sounded in her thoughts. So close and so clear, Kara was tempted to glance along the beach behind her as if she might see her sister standing there, her hair blowing in the breeze, her eyes sparkling with mischief. Marti would have encouraged Timmy to play with his father. Heck, she would have joined right in, always up for a challenge, always willing to try something new.

No one ever had to ask Marti if she was ready to have fun.

But how could she think of having fun at a time like this? How could Sam?

Guilt dug into her gut, and Kara crossed her arms tighter over her stomach. Was it so wrong for her to want him to see that Timmy would be better off with her? With the life they'd left behind in San Diego?

Timmy's future hung in the balance, and they had important decisions they needed to make before—oh, God, before Sam changed *her* mind. Before she started to believe that Timmy would be better off with Sam. With the life he could have here rather than the one they'd had in San Diego.

And he was close, closer than she'd ever thought possible after these last few days. Because even though Sam always started the day looking to have fun, he'd never once failed to teach Timmy a lesson along the way. Like when they went to dinner and he'd whispered for Timmy to run up ahead to open the door for her. Or the day at the local carnival when he'd won enough stuffed animals playing ball toss to open his own toy store and had Timmy give several away to kids who hadn't been so lucky. Or at the park, when an elderly man had trouble maneuvering his wife's wheelchair over a curb, and Sam had stepped in to help.

A cynical side of her wanted to believe it was all for show, but Sam's actions were too automatic, too easy to be anything but natural.

"All right, Timmy. Give it a big throw."

Kara watched her nephew draw back his arm and heave with all his might, but something clearly went wrong as the ball went straight up in the air and bounced a few feet behind him. Even knowing as little about football as she did, Kara still realized the ball was supposed to go forward.

"Whoa-ho! Way to break out a trick play and catch the defense by surprise. Now you're the running back, so grab the ball, race toward me and try to score."

She hadn't expected that—for Sam to put such a positive spin on Timmy's efforts, for him to praise instead of criticize. Her heart melted a little at the effort he was making and softened even further when Timmy grinned with pride like he'd known what he was doing all along.

He raced back for the ball. "I'm gonna score a—what's it called?"

"Touchdown."

"Yeah, a touchdown!"

Sam lunged at Timmy in a diving tackle, yet somehow only ended up catching a faceful of sand. He scrambled to his bare feet and ran after the little boy, his fingers jut missing him with every exaggerated grab. Only when Timmy veered too close to the edge of the water did Sam finally make the play. He caught Timmy around the chest and swung him up into his arms, lifting him high in the air.

Kara gasped at the sight of her nephew dangling eight feet off the ground and called out Sam's name. They both looked her way, greeting her with matching smiles, and her heartbeat slowed. They'd been having fun until she interrupted. Sam set Timmy down and murmured a few words before he sent the boy running across the beach to the bright blue cooler they'd brought along.

With Timmy off on his errand, Sam turned his attention back to Kara. His long stride carried him back across the sand, the look in his gaze making her feel stalked, hunted. Yet she stayed rooted to the spot. The soft grains seeping around her sandals might as well have been concrete.

"You called?"

Her heart pounding in her chest, Kara tried to remember what she'd been about to say. Something about the danger of falling… "You, um, need to be careful."

"Careful," he echoed.

"Yes. So no one gets hurt."

"You think I'm going to hurt you, Kara?"

Yes. "No. No! Not me—Timmy. You could have dropped him."

"You really think I'd let that happen?"

She'd seen the bulge of muscle in his tanned arms, the play and power of his chest and shoulders beneath the soft cotton T-shirt. Arms, chest and shoulders that were now mere inches away. If she reached out, she could run her fingertips over that soft cotton and discover that strength for herself. Kara swallowed. "No, you wouldn't have dropped him. But he was scared."

"I think *you* were scared."

"Well, I was worried that you'd frighten him and—"

"No." Sam cut her off with a shake of his head. "You were scared that Timmy was having fun."

She snapped her jaw shut, realizing it had dropped open at Sam's taunting words. "That's ridiculous! I'm not afraid of Timmy having fun."

"I think you're afraid of fun altogether."

Kara opened her mouth to argue, but the words didn't come. Because Sam was right? Because he'd nailed a truth about herself she didn't want to face?

Come on...it'll be fun...

The insidious whisper echoed through her thoughts, but it wasn't Sam's voice. Or her sister's. It was Curtis Graham's.

A far-off echo from a long time ago when she had given in. When she'd stopped focusing on her goals and dreams to focus on having *fun*. But the good times quickly came to an end when she found out the hard way that fun-loving boyfriends did not turn into fun-loving fathers the moment the pregnancy test came back positive.

After losing her daughter, Kara had quickly fallen back in line with the Starling way—work hard, study hard, strive to succeed. Her single-minded determination to focus on school had been the only thing to help her through the emotional devastation. She'd boxed away the pain and loss, but had her ability to have fun somehow gotten trapped there, too?

"That's not true," she protested weakly.

"Yeah?" Sam's cocky grin challenged her, but something more glittered in his eyes. A...gentleness, an understanding. Almost as if he somehow knew how her tightly laced control had become the stitches that held her tattered heart together.

Kara swallowed hard and took a half step back, ready to retreat, but he didn't let her. He caught her hand in his and tugged. "Prove it. Show me that you're not afraid to let loose." His trademark smile wavered ever so slightly, just enough for Kara to see the uncertainly beneath. "Show Timmy."

"Sam..."

His vulnerability slipped beneath her guard and the momentary weakness was her undoing as Sam took quick advantage. Grabbing her hand, he towed her relentlessly toward the water. "No, Sam! Wait!" Her heels dug into into the sand, but offered no resistance against the unrelenting pull. "It'll ruin my shoes!"

"Better get rid of 'em fast."

Recognizing he wasn't joking, Kara clumsily kicked off one sandal, then the other. Her toes sinking into the warm sand gave her an instant, almost exhilarating feeling of freedom. Still, she protested, "I'm not a good swimmer!"

Turning backward so he could face her, he laughed. "The water's only about knee-deep here."

She opened her mouth to argue, but the first cold slap of water against her legs stole the breath from her lungs. She gasped his name as her foot sank into the wet sand and she stumbled. The waves slapped at her knees, throwing her further off balance.

Sam caught her to his chest before she fell face first into the surf, and Kara reached out to grasp his T-shirt. Her hands dampened the material, and she had a crazy thought about the clear palm prints marking him as hers. His gaze dropped to her mouth and she licked her lips, tasting the salt of the ocean but hungering for more. For the salt of his skin. He murmured her name as another wave broke at her back, urging her body closer to his.

Her heart was pounding wildly in her chest. If Sam kissed her now, he'd have no doubt her desire for him was real. This attraction was about the two of them and had nothing to do with…Timmy.

Thoughts of the little boy distracted her, a cold mental shower dousing her heated thoughts, and this time she murmured a two-word denial. "Not now."

Sam blinked, looking as stunned as if he'd sleepwalked into the ocean and couldn't remember how he got there.

Another wave caught him slightly off balance, and before she let herself stop and think, Kara reached out and gave him a hard shove. Her timing must have been just right, the water's undertow and her push joined forces and toppled Sam into the water with a loud splash. He came up dripping wet, sputtering for air, and Kara took off running.

She barely made it out of the water before he caught up with her. He grabbed her by the hand and pulled, tumbling them both to the ground. The gritty sand rubbed against her shoulder blades and the back of her legs, and Sam was a contradiction of cold and hot above her—the icy chill from his soaked clothes and the irresistible heat coming off the muscular body beneath.

She longed to wrap herself around him, to cling to him like a strand of seaweed drifting in the water. Desire pooled in her belly, spreading out from there like ripples across a once-placid pond. She tried sucking in a calming breath, but her breasts brushed against his chest and any calm or placid thoughts were blown away by a storm of need. That hot-cold sensation seared her skin as the water soaking Sam's shirt seeped through hers. Her nipples tightened in response, aching for his touch, but her own protest was written in his heated gaze.

Not now.

She squealed when he shook his head like a water-logged dog and sent a spray of water from his dripping hair into her face. She was still breathless and laughing when he pulled her to her feet, the sound echoed a few yards away by Timmy who excitedly called out, "It's my turn now. Come chase me!"

"I wasn't sure I'd ever hear that sound," Sam murmured.

"It is good to hear him laugh."

He trailed a fingertip along her jaw, turning her face back to his. "Yeah, it is. But I wasn't talking about Timmy."

Chapter Nine

"I can't remember the last time I had so much fun."

Sam glanced over at Kara as he drove back toward town. Her clothes were still damp, but her hair had started to dry in soft waves that gently framed her face. His hands itched with the urge to reach out and run his fingers through the blond strands. Who would have thought her hair had a natural curl to it? And why did she go to so much effort to tame it?

Probably, Sam thought, for the same reason that her softly spoken words sounded like a confession of doing something wrong. Already signs of Professor Starling were returning as Kara tried to smooth her hair, her clothes. He could practically see the tension tightening her body as she sat up straighter, chin up, shoulders back, posture perfect.

It took all of Sam's control not to turn the minivan around and go back to find the laughing girl on the beach.

The one he'd held in his arms wanting to kiss her so badly he could taste it.

"Sometimes it's good to let go, forget about your worries and being an adult and just act like a kid again."

"I never really did things like that as a kid. Growing up was about going to school, working hard, getting grades that would mean acceptance into the right college."

The right kind of college. What would Kara think if she knew Sam hadn't gone to any college, right or wrong? That he'd barely graduated high school?

If you'd just study harder...

Heather's voice cut into his thoughts. His former high school girlfriend and almost-fiancée had focused on going to college, too. A dream that she—and, Sam had to admit, *he*—didn't think would ever come true. Not because she didn't have the grades, but because her family didn't have the money. He'd heard the longing in her voice as she spoke of going away to school, but he hadn't listened.

Instead he'd focused on the life he pictured—graduating from high school, finding a small apartment to share, and beginning their lives together. But that was before the offers of scholarships Sam hadn't known she'd applied for started coming in. Only then had he realized how different her picture of their future was compared to his.

"And then once I was at college..."

Her voice trailed off, and Sam glanced over. "More studying to get perfect grades?" he asked as he started to wonder about *her* childhood, about the pressure her parents had clearly placed on her. If she ever let herself stop thinking with that big brain and listened instead to the needs he knew existed within her beautiful body.

She was silent for a long time before she finally answered his questions—the one he'd asked and the ones he hadn't. "College wasn't all about hard work. For one semester, books and studying were the last thing on my mind after I—"

Met someone. Sam filled in the blanks. The vulnerability Kara tried so hard to hide told him she'd been hurt. He felt a surprising flicker of jealousy and a hotter flare of anger at the man responsible. He didn't want to reopen old wounds, but something told him they'd never really healed. "What happened?"

"I let loose. I had fun." A mocking lilt underscored the words, but the sarcasm wasn't thick enough to cover the pain and self-recrimination beneath. "It was—" Kara swallowed hard. "Things ended badly."

Sam longed to reach over and cover her white-knuckled fingers with his own. She was holding herself together so tightly, he worried the wrong move might cause her to shatter.

He shifted in the seat, wishing he were more like Drew, who always seemed to know the right thing to say. Sam had always been more about pushing buttons and provoking responses than soothing emotions.

"Not today," he pointed out.

"What?"

"You had fun today, and it didn't end badly."

She glanced over in surprise, her eyes widening a little as his words sank in. "You're right." Her lips rose in a teasing smile as she added, "Although the cynic in me wants to point out the day's not over yet."

"Which only makes me want to kiss you now," he retorted, gratified to watch the blush rise in her cheeks. "Just in case things go downhill from here."

She was still blushing fifteen minutes later when Sam pulled into the hotel parking lot. Timmy had slept the entire ride, not waking when Sam opened the back of the minivan. His lashes, a shade darker than his pale blond hair, rested against chubby cheeks that were slightly pink from time in the sun.

Sam figured the boy would wake up during the somewhat awkward transfer from the booster seat into his arms, but after a soft murmur, Timmy settled his head against Sam's shoulder. The warm weight in his arms seemed to seep straight into his heart in a way that was unfamiliar but not uncomfortable.

If anything, holding Timmy and inhaling the scent of surf, sand and little boy felt…right. Like the rush of love and protectiveness and joy when he and Timmy played together on the beach had felt right.

He reached out to shut the minivan door, but Kara beat him to it. "I'll get it," she said. "You have your hands full."

The words were simple enough on the surface, but a world full of complications and complexities swirled beneath them. He did have his hands full. Trying to get to know his son. Trying to figure out how to best be a father to the boy. Trying to figure out the role Kara would play in both of their lives.

He wanted her, Sam couldn't deny that. But sex always complicated a relationship and wasn't theirs complicated enough already? They both loved Timmy, they both wanted what was best for him, and yet they had completely different ideas of what that meant.

"Um, Sam…"

The tentative, female voice broke the moment, and Sam glanced over to see Nadine Gentry standing on the sidewalk a few yards away. Her red Rolly's apron was draped over her thin forearm, and she carried a to-go box from the diner.

"Hey, Nadine. How's it going?"

She gave a small shrug. "Okay. I, um, see that you're busy, but I just wanted to let you know that me and Darrell aren't together anymore."

"Can't say I'm all that sorry to hear it."

"Me, neither. I went to bail him out, you know, but then I thought about him being in jail, sitting behind bars, and pretty much figured he belonged there." Lifting her chin to a proud angle, she told him, "I talked to the sheriff about pressing charges."

"That's great, Nadine. That took a lot of courage."

"I don't think I could have done it if it wasn't for you."

Sam felt the back of his neck start to heat at the other woman's gratitude and the awareness of Kara silently watching the exchange. "I didn't really do anything."

"You were willing to stand up for me and for my son," Nadine said. "Thank you for that."

"You're welcome. Let me know if there's anything else I can do."

"Just help keep an eye on my boy." She gave a small smile as she nodded to Timmy still sound asleep against his shoulder. "That was a lot easier to do when Will was that age."

After saying good-night to Nadine, Sam shifted Timmy in his arms, half hoping the boy would wake up. Nadine's gratitude had made him feel uncomfortable, but to see Kara gazing up at him like he was some kind of hero…

The pride in her caramel eyes made him feel fifty feet tall, but when reality set in, when Kara saw him for who he really was, he was going to be in for one hell of a fall.

"Night, Timmy," Sam whispered as he tucked the stuffed dinosaur tighter beneath Timmy's arm.

Standing in the doorway to Timmy's room, Kara crossed her arms over her stomach. The little boy's request for

Sam to tuck him in had hit her hard. It was a change in the routine they'd established since Timmy had come to live with her.

Sam was becoming a part of Timmy's life. And a part of hers…

As Sam rose and turned away from the bed, his gaze locked on hers. The quiet intimacy of the moment grabbed hold of Kara and refused to let go. Such a simple thing—watching a father tuck his son into bed. The ritual was repeated by families every night the world over. But she and Sam weren't parents. Timmy was her family, and her focus needed to stay on him and not on Sam.

Sam…who had crossed the room to stand right in front of her. Sam…who was gazing down at her with enough heat for her to wonder if he'd read her thoughts about couples putting a child to bed before slipping between the sheets together…

"Wait!" Timmy called out, the urgency in his voice breaking the moment.

"What is it, buddy?"

A sliver of light shone into the bedroom, enough for Kara to see her nephew's wide eyes as he sat up in the middle of the bed. "Timmy?" Sam prompted. "What's wrong?"

"Nothing," he whispered faintly as he drew his dinosaur closer. "'Night."

Kara's heart ached a little at the combination of fear and bravery she saw in his face as he huddled beneath the covers and she stepped closer. She touched the hand Sam had wrapped around the handle. "I've been leaving the door open so it's not so dark."

Realization crossed his face as he glanced back at his son, and Kara bit her lip to keep from rushing to her nephew's defense. Her own parents had been far too logical to bother with nightlights when she'd been a child, unconcerned by their daughter's fear of the dark.

Nothing exists in the dark that isn't in the light.

Nothing but a little girl's fears and wild imagination….

"No worries, Tim." Reaching into his pocket, Sam pulled out his keys. "I bought a new flashlight not too long ago, and it came with this little light." Unhooking the small flashlight, no bigger than a cigarette, he said, "I put it on my keys because sometimes when I leave the garage at night and it's dark—"

"You get scared?" The little boy scooted to the edge of the bed, his eyes wide with shared sympathy.

Sam barely missed a beat. "Yeah, Tim, I get scared." Handing the flashlight to his son, he added, "But when I turn this on, it's not so scary anymore. Do you think it would help if you kept this with you tonight?"

"Uh-huh," Timmy's curls bounced against his forehead as he nodded. He clicked the small light on. "But what about you?"

"I've got the big light back at my shop, remember? I'll be okay."

It took a few more minutes to get Timmy tucked back into bed, the glowing flashlight within his reach. By then, his eyelids were getting heavy, and Kara knew he'd fall asleep quickly.

"Good night, Timmy."

"'Night, Aunt Kara. 'Night, Sam."

The little boy's sleepy voice floated across the room, and Sam froze outside the door. His hesitation was barely noticeable, and Kara might have missed it if she hadn't overheard his conversation with his father on the Pirellis' front porch.

"I know this hasn't been easy—not telling Timmy who

you are, but it's only been a few days," Kara murmured as she led the way into the suite's small living space.

"It's been four years," he countered. "Four years I've missed."

"That's not your fault."

"Isn't it? If I'd been a different kind of man, someone Marti trusted to be there for her, for Timmy, maybe she would have come to me. But Marti didn't trust me enough to tell me the truth. She didn't trust that I'd do the right thing."

"The right thing," she echoed. Having met his family, Kara didn't have any doubt about what the Pirellis thought was the right thing to do. But wrapping her head around the idea of a man with Sam's reputation settling down wasn't easy.

As if reading her mind, he added, "I had a great childhood, growing up here surrounded by family. It's the kind of childhood Timmy deserves, too, two parents living together, raising him together, under one roof. But the hell of it is, I'm not sure what I would have done if I had known Marti was pregnant. So maybe she was right not to trust me. Maybe she knew me better than I knew myself."

"Or maybe," Kara countered softly, "she didn't know you at all."

A wry smile twisted his handsome face. "Everything was fine when Marti thought I was some rich guy who could spend a couple hundred grand on cars. But once she found out I was nothing more than a simple mechanic, that was that."

His tone was matter-of-fact, but a trace of hurt lingered in his words. Sam Pirelli—vulnerable? It didn't seem possible. Yet Kara couldn't ignore the uncertainty she sensed in him, any more than she could stop the softening of her feelings for this man who was so much more than the simple mechanic he'd described.

"You can't blame yourself for a choice my sister never gave you the chance to make. It doesn't matter what you might or might not have done five years ago. All that matters is what you're doing now." Reaching up, she brushed her fingers against his jaw. The late-day stubble sensitized her skin, chasing goose bumps up her arm.

"You're a good man, Sam."

His broad shoulders rose and fell on a heavy sigh. "What I want," he admitted in a low murmur, "is to be a good father."

"What you did just now…that's what being a good father is all about."

Sam shook his head. "That was nothing."

"Not to a little boy who's afraid of the dark but doesn't want to admit it, it isn't."

She'd been the one to emphasize how smart Timmy was—a point that had been driven home so often during her own childhood. Intellect over emotion, mind over body. But no matter how bright he was, he was still a little boy who needed a man in his life.

Not just any man, but a father like Sam. A father who could encourage Timmy to run and play and live life outside of his head and the world of books and make believe. A father who could teach him how to stand up for himself but also to look out for the people around him. A father who could show by example how to grow from a good boy into a *good man*.

And wasn't that a twist of irony? Curtis's unwillingness to take responsibility had broken her heart years ago. And now—now Sam's willingness to do that very thing would tear Timmy from her arms, taking her best chance at being a mother with him.

To her embarrassment, Kara felt the hot press of tears at the back of her throat, and she tried to turn away before Sam could notice. But it was almost as if he didn't need to see her tears to know how she was feeling. His fingers curved around her shoulder and he turned her into his arms.

His T-shirt was slightly rough from the salt water, and he smelled of surf and sand and sunshine. The dunk he'd taken in the ocean had brought out the curl in his dark blond hair, making him look even more boyishly appealing. But the strength of the body pressed to hers was all man.

She whispered his name a moment before his lips claimed hers. She'd tried to convince herself their first kiss couldn't have been as good as she remembered, couldn't have been as powerful, couldn't have made her feel so much need or so needed. But this was all that and more, because behind this kiss was everything she'd learned about Sam since that first kiss. About his kindness, his patience, his vulnerability…

"Sam, I don't—I shouldn't do this." She whispered the words even as her fingers tightened in his sun-dried hair.

"Shouldn't?"

Kara shivered as he spoke the word against the fragile skin of her throat. "I don't want you to think I'm using you."

That got his attention, and he lifted his head far enough to meet her gaze. Desire darkened his eyes and quickened his breathing, but his voice was almost too even as he repeated, "Using me?"

"You said before you thought I was playing you, using the attraction between us against you…." She swallowed hard. "Ever since I came here, my mind has been racing. Should I tell you about Timmy? Should I keep quiet? What will happen if I do? Can I live with myself if I don't? All these thoughts, and I just want them to stop! I want to stop thinking and to just feel."

Sam was silent for a moment before he murmured, "Feeling is good. Feeling can be really good."

"But it's not fair to you!"

He chuckled as he lowered them both to the couch. "You have my permission. Use away."

She wasn't sure what he meant at first until he leaned back against the cushions, inviting her to…do as she pleased. Kara didn't let herself stop and think. Leaning forward, she brushed her lips against his mouth, the rough scrape of beard at his chin, the hollow of his throat. Tasting, feeling…all the while she explored the shape and size of the muscles hidden by his T-shirt. His shoulders, his chest, his stomach. The dry rasp of his breathing sounded in her ear as his body trembled and tightened beneath her fingers.

His hands gripped her hips but not once did they stray from that spot as he gave himself over to her, letting her be the one in charge just as he'd promised. And somehow it didn't matter that he wasn't touching her. She felt so in tune with his body, so connected to Sam, that she could almost experience his hands on her in every place she touched like some kind of phantom pleasure.

Her hands had just drifted lower when a soft cry carried out from the bedroom.

Kara froze, even as Sam reacted. He practically lifted her from the couch as he stood. Keeping her hand in his as his long strides led the way to the bedroom, he'd just reached for the doorknob when Timmy called out again. "Mommy!"

It was Sam's turn to freeze, but Kara had heard the heartbreaking cry before. As she pushed the door open, enough light spilled in from the hall for her to see Timmy sitting up in bed, his eyes wide but unfocused as tears streamed down his round cheeks.

She'd learned the hard way it was best not to wake him

but to try to soothe him back to sleep. It was a lesson she didn't have time to explain to Sam as he rushed ahead of her and tried to take his son into his arms. But the minute Timmy became fully awake, he started screaming and scrambled back against the headboard. "No! No! Go away. I don't want you. I want Aunt Kara!"

Chapter Ten

"Sam found out about Timmy before you could tell him?" Sympathy and a touch of horror filled Olivia's voice even from across the miles. "Ouch!"

"Well, I guess that's better than 'I told you so,'" Kara said as she watched Timmy from the small kitchenette. His head was bent over a piece of paper with colorful markers spread across the coffee table.

"But?" her friend prompted.

"You told me so."

Olivia only gave a small, smug chuckle before turning serious. "So what's he like? Now that you've gotten to know him?"

"He's—" Memories of last night's kiss swamped her, and Kara was glad her friend wasn't there in person, certain Olivia would read the truth behind the heat rising to her face. "He's trying to connect with Timmy."

"Trying? But not succeeding?"

"At first I didn't think so, but yesterday..." Kara filled her friend in on their day. "You should have seen Timmy running along the beach and heard how hard he was laughing."

She left out the way she, too, had gotten caught up in the game. She still couldn't believe she'd pushed Sam into the surf. Or how hard she'd been laughing as she stumbled in the loose sand, trying to make her escape, before Sam had tumbled them both to the damp and gritty beach. His gaze had roamed over her damp clothes, her windswept hair and pinked cheeks as if she was the most beautiful woman he'd ever seen, and Kara had thought sure he was going to kiss her.

But he hadn't.

The kiss had come later with no one around to see and only her own conscience to know how much further the kiss might have gone if not for Timmy's nightmare.

But she wasn't about to tell Olivia that either.

Focusing on Timmy instead, she said, "I never really thought about Timmy liking sports. He's always been so interested in reading and puzzles."

"Like you?"

"I know what you're thinking. That Timmy likes what's familiar to him." She'd seen the hurt on Sam's face when Timmy pushed him away after his nightmare. The little boy had clung to her, taking comfort in her arms and in the sound of her voice as she sang him back to sleep. He'd slept through until morning and woke up without seeming to remember the nightmare. His first question had been to ask when they were going to see Sam.

"There's nothing wrong with holding on to what's familiar," Olivia said. "But it's okay to spread your wings a little, too, and embrace something new. Someone new..."

Kara knew her friend was right, but she couldn't help the little twinge in her heart at the idea. Already Timmy seemed less like Marti's little boy and more and more like Sam's son.

"Besides, sweetie, it's not like Timmy can't like both sports and books. He doesn't have to pick one or the other." Her friend paused. "He can love both."

Kara closed her eyes on a sigh as her friend's point drove home. "Just like he can love both Sam and me."

"Wow! You know, I never thought of it like that."

"Oh, stop! That's exactly what you've been saying." Lowering her voice, she said, "But a choice *is* going to have to be made. Either Timmy comes home with me or he stays here with Sam."

"Or...*you* stay there with Timmy and Sam."

"That's—that's crazy," Kara argued as if the thought hadn't crossed her mind far more than she wanted to admit. "What am I supposed to do about my condo, my career? The department chair position? I've worked hard to get where I am."

A faint echo followed her words, coming not from the cell phone but from her own mind as she recognized nearly the same words her parents had said to her over a decade ago when she'd told them she was pregnant.

She would have given up anything—her full-ride scholarship, her perfect GPA, her future career—to have had the chance to be a mother to her little girl for more than a few, heartbreaking days.

Could she do the same now for Timmy?

Nothing about leaving the little boy felt right, yet in her heart she knew taking him away from Sam would be just as wrong.

"Do you really think I should consider moving up here for Timmy?"

"For Timmy...for you...and maybe even for Sam."

"Sam?" Kara echoed, startled, only to lower her voice even further when Timmy curiously glanced her way.

"Sam wouldn't have anything to do with my decision. He's Timmy's father, but that's all."

"Kara, I think we both know he's something more. I can hear it in your voice when you talk about him."

"Hear what?"

"There's this smile."

"That's ridiculous. It's impossible to hear a smile."

"Oh, really?"

"Really."

"Okay, genius, I'll bet you a hundred bucks that right now I'm hearing a frown."

"You're hearing annoyance."

"Okay, and when you talk about Sam, I hear happiness and interest and lust. Should I go on?"

"Please don't."

"Look, all I'm saying is to keep an open mind for a solution that isn't as cut-and-dried as Timmy choosing between you and Sam. Maybe there's a compromise where you all win."

After saying goodbye to Olivia with a promise to call again in a few days, Kara dropped her phone into her purse and rounded the short countertop separating the kitchenette from the small living room. "What are you working on, Timmy?"

"A picture for Sam."

Two figures with bright yellow hair held flashlights with beams shooting out like lasers. Dark scribbles crouched in the corners—monsters vanquished by the father-son duo. "That's great, Timmy."

"I'm gonna draw another picture of Sam's car. Sam said he'll take me for a ride. We'll go really fast with the top down."

Sam says... Timmy was still a little shy in Sam's presence, but he was full of stories, recounting what Sam said when he wasn't around. Yes, Timmy had clung to her after his nightmare the other night, and she knew how his rejection had hurt Sam. But Timmy had reached out for what was most familiar, most comforting.

If she hadn't been there, he would have turned to Sam. If she hadn't been there, Timmy would be far more open to talking to Sam instead of talking about him.

Kara swallowed. Was her presence hurting more than it was helping?

"And this one. It's a picture of you and me and Sam at the beach," Timmy was saying as he held out the drawing for her to see. Three stick figures ran along a tan beach, holding hands beneath a vivid blue sky. He'd given each character a bright red smile, a clear sign of the good time he'd had.

"You had fun at the beach, didn't you?"

"Uh-huh. It was—" Ducking his head, Timmy went back to coloring, pressing down hard enough that the marker squealed across the paper.

"It was what, Timmy?"

"It was like a real family with a mommy, a daddy and a little boy."

The softly spoken words sucked the air from Kara's lungs. Had she really thought Timmy wasn't old enough, wasn't smart enough to realize he didn't have a father? Yes, single-parent families were common these days, but that link, that connection of father, mother and child was still so important, so vital.... What had Sam said?

It's the kind of childhood Timmy deserved, too, two parents living together, raising him together, under one roof.

A real family.

Sam looked up at the quick knock on his office door. He'd come in to catch up on some of the paperwork that had piled up over the last week and also to make sure Will could handle working most of the weekend on his own. Neither of them had talked about their argument, and Sam was more than willing to let that sleeping dog lie.

"What's up, Will?"

"Sal Dougan's here." Bracing his skinny arms on either side of the open doorway, he leaned into the room. "He's got a flat on his van." The teen drummed his fingers against the frame. "He says he just wants to fix the one, but the other three are as bald as, well, as Sal is," he said with a huff of a laugh that quickly faded away. "I think he's worried he can't pay for the other ones. I thought you might wanna talk to him."

"Thanks, Will."

The boy nodded and stepped back from the doorway, but before Sam could pass by, he blurted out, "I was wrong the other day when I told you to stay out of my business. I mean, we're friends, right? And friends look out for each other."

"Yeah, they do."

Will dropped his head and scuffed the toe of his work boot along the vinyl floor. "My mom's pressed charges against Darrell. She says I might have to testify."

Poor kid. He did okay one-on-one, but he clammed up in front of a crowd. Sam could only imagine how nervous he'd be on a witness stand. "You'll do fine if it comes to that."

"Yeah." The teen lifted his head and grinned. "Oh, hey, I saw you'd started repainting the 'Vette, but I thought you were leaving her red?"

Sam breathed out a sigh, thinking of the soon-to-be shiny black sports car. "Sometimes plans change."

After leaving Kara's hotel room, he'd gone straight to the shop. He'd known he wouldn't be able to sleep.

Not with the memory of Kara's kiss replaying against Timmy's nightmare.

In a way, he felt as if he'd been the one dreaming. One minute Kara was clinging to him, kissing him with a passion and desire beyond anything he could have imagined. The next minute, his son was screaming and pushing Sam away.

God, that had hurt. He'd never known the punch a four-year-old kid could pack. If Kara hadn't been there, he didn't know what he would have done.

Standing outside the doorway last night, he'd watched as she rocked Timmy in her arms. The soft sound of her voice eased the tension from his little body. His shuddering breaths soon eased, and he'd drifted back to sleep.

The soft glow from the light in the hall had touched her profile as she leaned down and kissed Timmy's forehead. The complete and utter devotion on her face had stopped Sam's breath in his chest, and he'd had to face the question hovering outside his thoughts for the past few days. Would Timmy be better off with Kara than with him?

Staring at the 'Vette that he'd primed and sanded, he hadn't found an answer. But he had made a decision. He was still a little surprised he wasn't feeling a greater sense of disappointment, but putting his dream on hold felt right. He and Kara still hadn't talked about the future, but Sam knew one thing for sure. Whatever free time he had, he wanted to spend with Timmy—if not in Clearville, then in San Diego.

Sam's assistant, Will, greeted Kara as she and Timmy walked toward the open bay door of the garage. The teen wore a pair of coveralls and a red baseball cap pulled low over his forehead. "Sam's just finishing up with a customer, but he'll be glad to see you guys. Especially since you brought lunch from Rolly's," he said with an envious nod at the brown bags in Kara's hands.

"I asked one of the waitresses about Sam's favorite meal, and she said that you both like cheesesteak sandwiches."

"You got me one, too?"

"If you're hungry," Kara said, hiding a smile at the way the boy nearly snatched the bags from her hand.

"Starved!" Walking over to a shiny black truck, he dropped the tailgate to use for a makeshift seat and immediately dug in.

Kara lifted Timmy up beside the teenager and said, "I didn't think to bring any drinks."

"Sam has a vending machine inside the garage. I can go grab some sodas," the teen offered, but he already had his hands full of his sandwich.

"I'll go. Timmy, are you okay waiting out here?"

"Uh-huh." He eyed the second bag, most likely hoping to sneak a few of the fries she'd promised him if he ate his chicken strips.

"Okay. Do not let him eat all of the fries before I get back," she told Will and then pretended not to see the conspiratorial glance pass between the two boys.

Kara stepped from the bright sunlight into the shadowed interior of the garage, more than a little intimidated by all the tools and machinery she couldn't begin to name. The smell of motor oil, rubber and exhaust fumes filled the air. At the moment, all the equipment was silent, the cavernous space quiet enough for sound to carry from Sam's office.

"Thanks, Sam. I can't tell you how much I appreciate this."

"No problem. Those tires have been ready to go for a while now."

"Yeah, I know, but—"

"You have three kids riding in your van, Sal. There's no 'but' about that."

"I'll pay you back," Sal vowed.

"He does stuff like this all the time."

Kara spun around, startled by Will's voice. "I thought maybe you needed a hand with the drinks," he added.

The vending machine glowed in the corner. She thought of making up some story, but it was more than obvious she'd been listening to Sam's conversation. Still… "I didn't mean to eavesdrop."

Will shrugged. "It's no secret that Sal's had a hard time lately. He got laid off a while ago and hasn't found another job. It's up to him to support his family…" Will's voice trailed off as he glanced away with a frown. "Anyway, Sam's really good at looking out for people."

"I know." Over the past few days, Kara had seen the kind of man Sam was, the kind of father he could be—fun-loving, but caring, too. Able to teach his son about guy things like sports and cars, but more importantly, showing him how to be a man by the kindness and respect he gave his friends and family.

The sound of Sam's voice grew louder as Kara inserted the last of her quarters into the soda machine. His eyes widened and he grinned as he caught sight of her. He shook hands and said goodbye to Sal before heading her way. "Kara, what are you doing here?"

"Timmy and I brought lunch, and Will was giving me a hand with the drinks." Kara handed the final can to the teen who ducked away as if belatedly embarrassed by the talking he'd done. "If you're busy—"

"No, I was just finishing up. Besides, I'm never too busy for lunch with my son and his beautiful aunt."

Kara felt her face start to heat. It was ridiculous how easily he could fluster her with a single glance or a flirtatious comment. But there was something beneath the teasing look in his green eyes that made her think he meant every word.

"Timmy has a picture he wants to give you."

The one of Sam and Timmy together, battling the shadow monsters. Kara had left the picture of the three of them together, like a real family, back at the hotel. Of course out of sight wasn't out of mind. Not when she could still hear the sound of Timmy's voice, the longing in his words.

A daddy, a mommy and a little boy....

"I'd forgotten about that. The dozens of pictures I used to bring home to my parents..." Sam's voice trailed off, and Kara could see how much it meant to continue a tradition he'd had with his own parents. Hiding his emotions behind a laugh, he added, "Knowing my mom, she probably still has all of them tucked away somewhere for safekeeping."

"Your mom does seem like the sentimental type."

"Yeah, she is. In fact, I stopped by my parents' house earlier and picked up something for Timmy," he said as he guided her toward his office. Reaching into a drawer, he said, "Believe it or not, she saved this." A superhero-shaped nightlight rested in his outstretched hand. "It was mine as a kid. My brothers gave me such a hard time for being afraid of the dark. At least Timmy doesn't have to worry about *those* monsters as well as the ones under the bed."

"He's going to love it." And she should have remembered to bring one from home. Maybe that would have kept him from having the nightmare in the first place. "About last night—"

Sam's eyebrows rose, and Kara realized why as his gaze dropped to her lips. "I, um, mean about Timmy's nightmare."

The heat in his gaze cooled as he gruffly asked, "Does that happen a lot?"

"A few times since we've been here."

"And what about before you came?" Kara hesitated long enough for Sam to make his own conclusions. "It didn't, did it? Timmy wasn't having nightmares until you brought him here."

"No, that's not true! He did have nightmares back home, but being in his own bed, surrounded by his own things, he settled down easier," she admitted. "The only reason Timmy reached out to me last night is because he's more comfortable with me."

"Just how often did Marti leave Timmy with you?" Sam asked softly.

Startled by his change in subject, she protested, "That's not why—"

"I'm not judging her, Kara." A slight wince crossed his features. "Or at least, I'm trying not to, but I want to know what Timmy's life was like with Marti…and with you."

"She was my little sister." Lifting her hands in a helpless gesture, she added, "She was young and beautiful, and she liked going out."

"You make it sound like you were some kind of old-maid aunt. You're young, beautiful…why weren't you the one going out while Marti took care of her own child?"

"I just didn't. And when—if I'd been in Marti's shoes, I would have wanted someone to be there for me, the way I was for her. I never minded watching Timmy. Never. I loved every minute."

She'd lived for those phone calls from Marti, hoping to hear the excitement in her sister's voice, knowing it meant she had a date planned. Taking care of her nephew had filled Kara's empty arms and a small part of the hole in her heart left by her daughter's death. Nothing and no one could ever replace Ella, but her nephew's birth had helped heal the hurt more than time or the way she'd thrown herself into school and her career ever had.

"I know how much you love him and how much he loves you." He dropped his head but not before Kara had seen the pain in his eyes. "You're the closest thing he has to a mother. That's why I don't know how…I can't…"

"Hey, you two, hurry up!" Will called out from the front of the garage. "Before me and Timmy eat all the food!"

Sam exhaled a breath as if the interruption had given him a reprieve from what he might have said. "We should get out there."

Kara followed him down the hall and outside, barely managing to put one foot in front of the other. For a second, she'd been so sure Sam had made up his mind about the decision facing them, the one they'd agreed not to talk about, and that hovered around them like early morning fog coming off the ocean.

Had Sam really been about to say he couldn't take Timmy from her?

"Sam!"

Timmy pushed off the tailgate as he caught sight of his father. He rushed over with a wide grin and one of the still-wrapped sandwiches in his hands. A sandwich he exchanged for the nightlight and a piggyback ride back to the truck. His laughter drifted across the lot, and the hope floating through Kara's heart sank.

I don't know how...I can't...

"I don't know how either, Sam," she whispered beneath her breath. "And I can't take him away from you."

Maybe there's a compromise where you all win.

Whatever that compromise was, she hoped she and Sam could find it soon.

Chapter Eleven

For years, Sam and his brothers had met at Rolly's Diner on Mondays for lunch, but this was one get-together he wasn't looking forward to. Plastering a fake smile on his face, he greeted his older brothers at their large table in the back of the diner. "If it isn't my two favorite brothers!"

Grabbing the laminated menu from his oldest brother's hands—Sam didn't know why Nick bothered looking at it when he ordered the same burger and fries every time they came—he asked, "How are the wedding plans coming along?"

As a stall tactic, that line wasn't his best. As happy as Nick was to be marrying Darcy Dawson, wedding talk wasn't going to be enough to save Sam from the grilling he knew his brothers had in store for him. By the end of the meal, chances were good he'd end up with more scorch marks on his hide than on Nick's well-done burger.

But the questions his brothers were bound to ask were

the same ones that had been plaguing him since he found out about Timmy. Questions that weren't getting any easier to answer.

"You're asking the wrong member of the wedding party that question," Drew cut in before Nick could respond. "Nick is leaving everything in his beautiful bride's hands. And in Mom's and Sophia's and Hope's."

Nick shrugged at the teasing. "I wouldn't have it any other way. I get to marry the woman I love without having to be in on every decision about invitations and napkins and place settings. My only job is making sure you two clowns show up at the church on time."

"I think that's more the other way around. We'll be the ones propping you up when you're ready to hit the floor."

"Not a chance," Nick vowed with enough certainty to send a streak of something Sam refused to call envy shooting straight through his heart.

They talked for a few more minutes about the upcoming bachelor party, but not even that topic kept Nick from circling back to Sam. "Have you told Timmy you're his father yet?"

Sam shook his head. "He's still getting to know me. Timmy's been through a lot already. We can't just drop something like this on him. Kara and I agreed to take a few days for me to get to know Timmy before we talk about the future."

"You're going to have to tell him eventually," Nick pointed out.

"I know," Sam said, fighting the urge to turn Nick's words into a criticism by instantly turning defensive. "But Kara and I agreed the best thing is to take it slow."

"How slow?"

"What do you mean?"

"Are you telling him next week? Next month? Next year?"

"It isn't something you can put on a timeline!"

"Maybe you can't," his brother muttered.

"What's that supposed to mean?"

"Sam—" Nick cut off whatever he was going to say and started again. "You said yourself Kara loves Timmy, and you can just bet that a woman like that is already making plans for *her* future with him."

"We both agreed," Sam argued, but Nick just shook his head, disappointment darkening his gaze.

Irritated, Sam fought against arguing back. Against defending himself…and Kara. He knew Nick thought he was being naive, foolishly trusting in the woman who posed a threat to his relationship with his child. But that was more about his big brother's past with his ex. Carol had walked out on Nick and their daughter only to change her mind and want back into Maddie's life.

But Kara wasn't like that. Sam could trust her. He did trust her.

The question was whether or not he could trust himself. Would he have the strength to do the right thing—even if that meant letting Timmy go?

"I don't get it, Sam. I don't understand why you aren't fighting with everything you've got for that boy." Frustrated by the lack of response, Nick pushed away from the table despite Drew's protests. "I'm going to leave now before I say something I'll regret."

Sam let out a bark of a laugh. "Come on, Nick. When'd you ever let something like that stop you?"

"Fine," his older brother bit out. "This whole live-for-the-day, never-take-life-seriously attitude of yours? I thought maybe, just maybe, it was some sort of facade.

That when push came to shove, you could man up and take responsibility when it mattered. Looks like I was wrong."

Nick's exit wasn't dramatic enough to cause the entire restaurant to fall silent, but Sam felt as if it had. Or maybe the doubts swirling through his mind were so loud, they drowned out the normal sounds of silverware clanking against plates, orders being called out from the counter and the laughter and conversation from the tables around them.

"So," Drew's calm voice cut through the din, and Sam blinked, refocusing on his brother. "Was Nick wrong?"

Sam sucked in a breath. It probably shouldn't have surprised him that Nick and—judging by the knowing expression on his face—Drew had seen through him so clearly. Had seen that his good-time-guy-grin was little more than a mask. But if both his brothers knew—hell, maybe the only one he'd been fooling was himself.

"Don't you know?" Sam finally asked wryly. "Big brother's never wrong."

"That's pretty much what he's been saying our whole lives. Not that I'm about to tell him it's true."

"This isn't about being afraid of responsibility or not wanting to take fatherhood seriously. I know how serious this is. How important it is to do the right thing here."

"But?" Drew prompted when Sam bit back his next words.

"I'm not so sure that Timmy living here—living with me is the right thing." After briefly explaining about Timmy's nightmare and the way the little boy had pushed him away and clung to Kara, he said, "He's already lost his mother, but the way Kara's stepped in..."

He'd never had the chance to see Marti with Timmy and maybe he wasn't being fair to his ex-girlfriend, but Sam couldn't imagine that she'd loved Timmy any more than Kara did.

"I've been—" Sam cut himself off before saying out loud the thought that had been playing through his mind. An idea he'd barely acknowledged because it was too crazy to consider, wasn't it? "I've been thinking about asking Kara to stay."

His heart was pounding in his chest just hearing the words, and he looked up to try to gauge his brother's reaction. Drew had always been the type to play things close to the vest, but Sam expected a hell of a lot more than a slight eyebrow lift, considering the bombshell he'd just dropped.

"It's crazy, right?" he asked without waiting for Drew to respond. "I mean, just because I ask doesn't mean she'll say yes. Kara has a life in San Diego. A career. She's a college professor, for God's sake. Is she really going to give that up for—" *Me?*

Sam cut off the word before he could say it. This wasn't about him, about Kara's feelings for him, or God help him, his feelings for her. "For a life here in Clearville? Even if it does mean being a mother to Timmy."

"I guess that depends," Drew said finally.

"On what?"

"Are you asking her to stay because you need her help or because you need her?"

"I don't—I don't know what you mean."

Drew's knowing look called him a liar, but all he said was, "You might want to think about it. And if Kara doesn't give the right answer, it might be because you asked the wrong question."

Kara wasn't sure what to think when Sam asked her to meet him at his apartment before their planned night of pizza and a movie. The animated feature was geared toward families, and it was one Timmy had already seen. Like most kids, though, he could watch his favorites dozens of times without getting bored. She'd teased Sam about the movie choice, asking about the last cartoon he'd seen.

"I don't remember the last one," he'd confessed before adding, "but I'll remember this one."

The first movie he'd take his son to, but it certainly wouldn't be the last. Sam and Timmy had a whole future of 'firsts' ahead of them. Everything from Timmy's first day at kindergarten, his first lost tooth, his first role in a school play. Firsts Kara had always thought she would be a part of. Firsts she still longed to be a part of. If not in San Diego, then here in Clearville…

Her conversation with Olivia circled through her mind.

Do you really think I should move here for Timmy?

For Timmy...for you...and maybe even for Sam.

Could she do it? Give up everything and move to Clearville?

She glanced down at Timmy, his small palm tucked into her free hand, and realization swept over her. She wouldn't be giving up anything that mattered. Her heart was with the little boy at her side, and she was beginning to fear, with the man opening the door to greet them.

Sam's emerald eyes shined as he took in the sleeveless dress she'd bought at a small boutique on Main Street. The soft pink-and-white swirled pattern wasn't what she would normally buy, but the dress had fit her slim curves perfectly—something the heat in his gaze confirmed better than any dressing-room mirror ever could.

"Hi," she greeted him almost shyly, nervous butterflies dancing in her stomach as if this were a first date.

"Hi, Sam," Timmy piped up at her side.

A first date with a four-year-old chaperone, Kara thought.

"We brought you a present," Timmy said.

"Oh, yeah? What is it?"

"You hafta open it and see."

"I can't wait." Taking the large blue-and-white striped bag from her hand, he held out an arm for the two of them to enter his small apartment. The living area had a decidedly masculine feel with earth-tone furniture, a well-used coffee table and an enormous flat-screen television. But a few pieces of art decorated the other walls, and a burgundy throw and matching pillows brightened the tan couch and loveseat. Compliments of his mother, he had already told her. Timmy raced inside, giving Sam time to lean close and whisper, "You look amazing. Almost too good for going to see some kids' flick."

"Only 'almost'?" she asked, surprised to hear the flirtatious words coming from her mouth.

Sam made a sound of agreement. "Any better and I'd be tempted to forget all about the movie."

Her heart skipped a beat as his gaze dropped to her lips, and she knew if they'd been alone, he would have kissed her. A long-silent, reckless part of her wished he would anyway. But she had to be content with knowing how much he wanted to.

"So, what's this for?" he asked as he lifted the bag.

"Is it your birthday?" Timmy asked, peering inside when Sam set the present on the coffee table and sat down on the couch.

"Nope, not my birthday."

As he reached past the blue tissue paper, Kara sat down beside him. "Consider it a belated Father's Day present," she said softly.

Sam held her gaze for a long moment before he lifted out the first mahogany-colored frame and stared at the photo behind the glass. He was silent for so long, Kara couldn't stop the words spilling out to fill the gap. "When I was at your parents' house, I saw all the baby photos of you and the rest of your family. It didn't seem right that Timmy wasn't there." She swallowed hard as those words took on greater meaning. "Anyway, that's a picture I took at the hospital right after Timmy was born. I had two copies made—one for you and one for your parents."

Rubbing a thumb over the glass, Sam murmured, "I can't believe how small he was."

"Just over eight pounds."

Realizing the present wasn't anything as interesting as toys, Timmy sank down on the carpet to play with one of his plastic dinosaurs. It wasn't much privacy. Just enough for Sam to lean close and press a soft kiss to her lips. "Thank you," he murmured as he brushed a lock of hair behind her ear.

"You're welcome."

"I've got something of a surprise for Timmy, too."

"For me?" Eyes lit with excitement, the little boy abandoned his Jurassic world to scramble to his feet.

"Yep, come take a look," Sam said with a squeeze to Kara's hand before he carefully set the picture frame aside.

With her lips still tingling from his kiss, Kara wasn't sure what to expect when Sam led them down a short hall that obviously led to a bedroom and opened the far door. The space had clearly been used for storage and a makeshift guest room, with a slightly sagging futon beneath the window and a bookshelf lined with sports equipment. But the center of the room was filled with toys. Cars and trucks and trains. Actions figures frozen midbattle. Board games in beat-up boxes with the corners duct-taped together.

Sam was watching Timmy, waiting for his reaction, but Timmy froze in the doorway before looking up with his forehead wrinkled in confusion. "Do you have a little boy like me, Sam?"

Kara stood close enough to feel the impact of those

words on Sam. His entire body tensed, his muscles trembled with the effort of holding back the words he wanted to say. *Not like you—you. You are my little boy.*

She pressed a hand to her chest where her emotions were playing a heartbreaking game of tug-of-war.

Tell him, Sam.

No! Don't tell him—if you do, he won't need me anymore. Neither of you will...

Though the selfishness of her own thoughts nearly tore her up inside, she couldn't help hoping Sam would stay silent for just a little longer. She didn't know where he found the strength, but somehow Sam managed a smile for his son.

"Actually, these are some toys from when I was a little boy. After I picked up that nightlight from my mom, she went through and found some more of my old toys. I liked cars and trucks when I was a kid, but check this out." Sam grabbed a new, unopened box off the bookshelf. "This is Robosaurus. It's a machine and—"

"A dinosaur," Timmy breathed out as he held up his hands for the toy.

"Yeah, a dinosaur." Sam had recovered enough from the earlier moment to grin down at his son, and their matching smiles, the pure delight on Sam's face, made it easy for Kara to realize how his family had realized in a glance that Timmy was his son.

"Isn't it great? I got those, too." He swept an arm at another stack of boxes—ones with pictures of different-colored cars and trucks, all decked out with racing stripes and decals emblazoned on the front. "They're models. I loved putting them together as a kid, and your aunt told me that you like puzzles."

"And you liked cars." He'd been trying all along to find a way to connect with Timmy, but this time, he'd sought out common ground. Something they would *both* enjoy. Their eyes met over the little boy's head, his green gaze searching hers.

"It's great, Sam, really."

The room was a better mattress, a single dresser and cartoon-covered comforter away from being the perfect room for a little boy. The perfect room for Timmy.

Sam's brows lowered as if seeing through her too-bright enthusiasm but the ring of his cell phone interrupted, and he offered a quick apology. "It might be someone needing a tow." But as soon as he answered the phone, Kara read the concern on his expression and knew this wasn't anyone calling for roadside assistance.

With a promise to be right there, he snapped the phone shut. After seeing that Timmy was still focused on the new toys, Sam led Kara into the hallway. "That was Hope. Jake's taking Sophia to the emergency room. She fainted, and they're worried about her and the baby. She'd been having some kind of contractions, but she's still not due for months…."

Contractions...early labor...a baby born too small to survive...

Kara swallowed hard at Sam's words. Shadows closed in around her, but she read the fear in his taut expression and pushed the memories from her past back into their dark corners.

"Go, Sam. Be with your family."

Reaching out, she grasped his hands and gave a squeeze. He turned his wrists to lace his fingers through hers, his palm warm and rough against her cold, clammy skin. His throat worked in a rough swallow before he gruffly said, "You know, my sister's always been the runt of the family, but she packs a mean punch. She's tougher than she looks. She's going to be okay. Everything's going to be okay."

Determination filled his voice, refusing to accept anything other than a healthy, happy outcome, but he couldn't promise that. Bitter experience had taught Kara all the wishing in the world couldn't keep heartbreaking loss at bay. How many times had she prayed for her daughter to fight, to live, for the doctors to supply a miracle to keep Ella alive? How long had she waited for someone, anyone, to tell her everything would be okay?

Those words had never come, and yet, somehow, hearing them from Sam all these years later soothed a small amount of the pain inside her. Blinking back tears, she repeated, "You should go, Sam."

"I don't know how long…"

"Timmy and I will wait for you here." Worry clouded his gaze, and she echoed back to him. "Everything's going to be fine."

Using their joined hands to pull her close, he lowered his head for a quick, hard kiss. Her last statement seemed to echo in the silence he left behind, and for the first time in a long time, Kara found herself praying the words would come true.

Chapter Twelve

Sam spotted his family instantly in the hospital's small waiting room. Huddled together in one corner, their faces reflected his own fear and concern. A quick glance confirmed the entire Pirelli clan, along with Hope Daniels, was there. He didn't see his brother-in-law in the group, which had to mean Jake was in the back with Sophia. Was that good news? Sam wondered. Or bad?

"I got here as soon as I could. Have you heard anything? Is Sophia—are Sophia and the baby okay?"

His mother reached up to give him a hug. The scent of warm vanilla surrounding her was as familiar as it was comforting. "We haven't heard yet. The doctor promised to update us as soon as possible." She looked at her husband and all three of her sons. Sam guessed that Nick and their dad had already tried storming the reception desk more than once.

"We just want to know what's going on," his father said,

his whole demeanor more serious and somber than Sam could recall seeing.

"I know. We all do," his mother said. "But we have to give the doctors a chance to do their jobs."

Sam wasn't sure how much time passed as they took turns pacing the small waiting room. Every moment dragged by until ten minutes seemed like an hour, and yet trapped in that slow-motion world, he swore his parents aged a year. If someone didn't tell them something soon—

His mother's gasp interrupted his thoughts. "Jake! How are they?"

Sam turned in time to see his brother-in-law step into the waiting room. Jake dragged his hands over his face and whispered, "They're okay. They're going to be okay."

His family erupted into relieved cheers, but even as Sam absorbed the blow to his back from Nick, his eldest brother's version of a hug, he focused on his brother-in-law. No doubt Jake had been a rock for Sophia, strong and steady for the both of them. For the three of them. But now, with the good news delivered, he looked ready to collapse.

"Do they know what happened? The contractions—"

Jake shook his head at his mother-in-law's unfinished statement. "According to the doctors, the contractions are normal and not something to worry about." His dark frown seemed to say *he* would decide what was worth worrying about when it came to his wife and baby.

"But she fainted." Even dressed in her usual bright, flowing clothes, Hope appeared pale and subdued. "There has to be some reason why."

"She's suffering from hypotension—low blood pressure. That's what caused the dizziness and the blurred vision she had right before she fainted. They're giving her some IV fluids right now and want her to take it easy for a few days."

"She won't have to lift a finger," their mom vowed. She

and the rest of the family immediately started working out a schedule for someone to be at Sophia's side at all times, giving Jake the chance to slip away.

Sam followed his brother-in-law over to the windowed wall overlooking the parking lot. "Are you okay, man?"

Sam had never questioned Jake's willingness to love Sophia's child—a child not biologically his own—but if he had, the relieved tears in the other man's eyes would have answered him.

"I keep thinking about what could have happened if I hadn't been there." As a private detective, Jake could make his own hours, but he also had to make frequent trips out of town.

"You were," Sam argued. "That's what counts. You were right here when Sophia and the baby needed you."

That's what counts.

As his mother pulled Jake into another hug, Sam's own words echoed through his mind with a certainty he hadn't felt in a long time. Being there for Timmy was what mattered most. His concerns hadn't disappeared, but the desire to raise his son, to be at his side when the boy needed him, overrode those worries.

Another slap on the back brought the waiting room back into focus as Drew said, "Good news, huh?"

"The best." And looking around at his whole family gathered in support of his sister, Sam knew this was the life he wanted to share with his son. Not a few weeks here and there. Not over spring break or summer vacation. He wanted a full-time future with Timmy.

The idea settled into his chest comfortably. A perfect fit as if his heart had already accepted what his mind had struggled to believe. He and Timmy belonged together. Father and son…

He could picture it so clearly, and yet in his heart, he

knew the image was incomplete. Kara belonged there, too. By Timmy's side and maybe, if Sam were lucky enough to convince her, in his arms.

"This isn't about you," Kara whispered, using the mantra like a shield to keep memories of the past at bay.

After Sam left, she'd turned her focus to Timmy, making a game out of raiding Sam's refrigerator to see what they could find for dinner. The little boy had wanted to feast on the containers of cookies and ice cream they'd found in the freezer. Kara wasn't surprised—she already knew father and son both had a sweet tooth. But she'd also found several man-sized meals in the freezer, compliments of Sam's mother, she was sure.

After she and Timmy shared a pot-roast dinner, they'd gone back to the toys, where Timmy had thoroughly examined each one before, not surprisingly, wanting to play with the dino-robot. Kara never would have thought keeping a smile on her face and the right amount of energy and excitement in her voice could be so draining, but by the little boy's bedtime, she was exhausted. She was able to coax Timmy onto the futon, telling him that they were having a sleepover at Sam's and fumbling through some kind of explanation when he asked where she'd be sleeping.

But now, huddled in a corner of the couch, with Timmy finally asleep, Kara could no longer fight off the images of the past. Relentless memories forced their way around her like an angry mob, jostling her from side to side, ready to knock her down and trample her beneath the unrelenting pressure.

The emergency room…doctors and nurses rushing in and out…the panic and fear clutching at her as she prayed for her little girl….

Kara lowered her hand from the locket she wore around

her neck to her stomach. Perfectly flat now all these years later, but she could still remember how big she'd felt during those last weeks, how excited to feel the life moving inside, how she'd wished for someone to share that joy with her...only to later realize it was better that she'd been on her own. Better that no one else had to suffer the loss.

But Sophia wasn't alone. She had a large, loving family and caring friends to support her....

The same large, loving family Timmy would have if he stayed in Clearville.

Caught up in her thoughts, Kara started at the sound of the lock turning. Sam was back. Jumping up from the couch, she met him before he'd taken more than a step over the threshold. "How's Sophia? And the baby?"

The smile he gave was all the answer she needed, but he added, "They're going to be okay. The doctor's keeping Sophia overnight just to make sure, but she and the baby are going to be fine."

The wave of relief that washed over her was so strong, and yet not quite strong enough to keep the old sorrow at bay. "That's great, Sam. I'm so happy for your family."

She whispered the last words, barely able to get them past the lump in her throat, and Kara knew she had to leave before she broke down.

Sam's smile faded into a concerned frown as he ducked his head to get a better look at her face. "Kara, what's wrong?"

"I just—I should go."

His brows lowered. "Go? What about Timmy?"

"He's sound asleep. I'd—I'd hate to wake him. He can stay here tonight. With you. I'll come back in the morning before he gets up."

"What if he has another nightmare? What if he needs you?"

"He needs you, too, Sam. All you have to do is hold him, tell him everything's going to be okay…."

Reaching out, he brushed a strand of hair from her face. His fingertips grazed the dampness on her cheek and only then did Kara realize she was crying.

She tried to slip away, but Sam wouldn't let her go. Wrapping his arms around her, he pulled her tight and cradled her against his chest. "Everything's going to be okay."

His voice was a low, soothing murmur. She could feel the warmth of his body through his cotton shirt, hear the strong steady beat of his heart, and oh, how she wanted to believe every word he said.

"Sam."

She tried to pull back far enough to meet his gaze only to give a soft gasp when her necklace caught on one of the buttons on his shirt. They both reached up to untangle the chain, their fingers brushing. Her heart skipped a beat at the simple touch and then slammed against her rib cage as she realized she'd left the locket open and Sam was staring at the picture inside.

She felt the blood drain from her face. She snapped the locket closed, her hand fisted around the tiny gold oval, but it was too late. Too late to hide from the memories she tried so hard to keep locked away, not because she was ashamed, but because even after so many years the loss was still so hard to face.

"Kara." Cupping her cheek in his palm, Sam lifted her chin until she met his gaze. Questions and answers swirled in his green eyes, and she braced herself, but instead of asking, he simply said, "I'm so sorry." Compassion and understanding filled his voice.

He wrapped his hand around her closed fist until her fingers started to loosen. Until the past stopped being something to hide and protect and became something she was finally ready to share.

Opening the locket between them, she gazed down at her baby girl's face, so fragile, so small, nearly hidden beneath the tubes and wires hooked to the machines that had failed to keep her alive. "Her name was Ella Marie Starling. She was my daughter, and she lived for thirteen days, seven hours and twenty-two minutes."

Sam guided her back to the couch and sank down on the cushion beside her. "Do you want to tell me about her?"

"It's been so long," she whispered.

"Then maybe it's time," he said gently.

"It was my sophomore year in college," Kara began. Her second year in, and she'd been struggling. Her parents had been disappointed with a less than perfect grade in calculus. In every conversation, they expressed their disapproval of her major. Teaching elementary school wasn't prestigious enough for her surgeon parents. At the time, Kara had held firm to her dream of teaching little kids, looking forward to the day when she could open their eyes to the worlds of reading and writing. But deep down, she was afraid she might eventually give in to her parents' demands—and lose herself in the process.

"I'd been working so hard, and yet it wasn't enough. Nothing ever seemed to be enough, and one night a friend invited me to a party. I'm not sure who was more surprised when I said yes. That's where I met Curtis. He was smart and funny and popular. I never thought he'd look twice at me, but he did.

"I fell for Curtis hard. For the first time in my life, something meant more to me than school and study and preparing for my future."

"And then you got pregnant."

Kara nodded. "I actually thought everything would be

okay. Curtis was only one semester away from graduating, so by the time the baby was born, he'd be working full-time. He already had a job lined up at a nearby investment firm. I still had two years to go, but I thought I could go to school part-time those first few years. After that, our baby would have been old enough for daycare or preschool, and I could start teaching. I thought it would all work out.

"But Curtis didn't want to have anything to do with marriage or fatherhood. This was his last year of college and he was set to have the time of his life. Part of me couldn't even blame him for his reaction. That always-ready-for-a-party side of his personality was what attracted me in the first place. So how could I fault him for being who he was?"

Kara was briefly aware of Sam tensing at her side, but all he said was, "What happened after that?"

"I still thought things would work out okay. Going to school and taking care of a baby on my own wouldn't be easy, but I thought with a little help I could do it." The little help she'd expected from her parents had ended up being very little indeed.

"I was studying for midterms when the first pains started. I was still months away from my due date, so I thought it had to be something else. Anything else. But then the contractions started and they didn't stop. I was rushed to the hospital, but nothing they tried worked...." Kara released a shuddering breath. "And that's when Ella was born. She was so small, so weak..."

Sam took her hand, and she gripped it, grateful for the anchor he offered. She could feel his strength, his support, his caring, everything she'd needed all those years ago.

Everything she still needed now, Kara realized. After Ella, she'd stopped counting on other people, thinking her independence and self-reliance meant she was strong. But all it meant was that she was a coward, too afraid to open her heart and let anyone inside.

"After Ella was gone, my friends tried to help, but they seemed to think I should have been relieved. Not that they used those words, saying things like 'it wasn't meant to be' instead. My parents said the best thing to do would be to put it all behind me, so I went back to school, aced my midterms, and picked up where I'd left off, as if nothing had changed. But everything had, and I just didn't realize it.

"Later that semester, I was supposed to observe teachers in a school setting, and it took everything I had to set foot inside that elementary school. To see all those children, to look at their beautiful, happy faces and wonder. Is that what Ella would have looked like her first day of kindergarten? Is that how tall she would have been in first grade? Would she have wanted to wear her hair in those braids when she was in second grade? And I knew I couldn't do it. I couldn't be around children every day, thinking of all the steps in her life that she'd never had the chance to take. So I went back to school and to studying and ended up teaching college."

"And what about when Marti got pregnant and Timmy came along? Anyone can see how much you love him, but was that hard on you?"

"Somehow, it wasn't. Maybe because she had a little boy or maybe because he was Marti's child. I'm not sure. But I loved Timmy from the start. He was always his own person and never a substitute for Ella. Marti getting pregnant gave me the chance to be an aunt, and it's been a wonderful experience. One that helped me heal and took away some of the pain of losing my daughter. I was…content."

"But then Marti died."

"Yes. I never would have wished for that. Ever. But once she was gone, and Timmy needed someone, needed me, those old dreams of motherhood came back. I wanted to protect him, but I also wanted to protect myself." She sighed and turned to him. "I'm sorry, Sam. For not being up front with you right away and—"

"It's okay, Kara. I understand. Better now that you've told me about Ella, but even before, I knew you were looking out for Timmy. I can't blame you for that. It's my fault Marti didn't trust me enough to tell me about Timmy."

"That's not true," Kara argued, ready to tell him the reality she'd had to face over the last few days. Despite his fun-loving attitude, Sam was very much a man a woman could trust. She knew that, and her sister must have known it, as well. "Marti's decision wasn't about you. Or even about Timmy. It was all about her."

"What do you mean?"

"Everything you said about Timmy deserving a childhood with two parents living together, raising him together, under one roof, I think that's the very reason Marti *didn't* tell you."

"You mean she wanted to be a single mom?"

Guilt weighed against her chest, a feeling of disloyalty to her sister's memory pressing hard, but Kara couldn't let Sam keep thinking he was to blame. "I don't know if she wanted to be a single mom, but she definitely wanted to stay single. Her decision had nothing to do with you. None of this has been easy on you, and you've been so great. So patient and understanding with Timmy." Kara gave a small laugh. "And with me."

"Don't make me into too much of a saint," he warned gruffly as he leaned back against the couch cushions and pulled her into his arms.

Resting her head against his chest, Kara could hear the strong, steady beat of his heart. He didn't need to worry. She didn't want a saint. She just wanted Sam.

* * *

Sam hadn't experienced many sleepless nights in his life, at least not ones that didn't include partying and having a good time. But as enough light started seeping into the living room for him to clearly see the rafters he'd been staring at for the past few hours, he realized he hadn't slept for more than twenty minutes at a shot. He didn't know how many times he'd jerked awake in a panic, certain the boy—or the woman—sleeping beneath his roof needed him.

He knew Kara hadn't expected to spend the night, but once she fell asleep in his arms, he hadn't had the heart to wake her. The emotional evening had left traces behind—circles beneath her eyes and faint lines on her forehead. Sam wasn't sure how long he held her. Long enough, he supposed, that he never wanted to let her go. Once he realized she wasn't going to wake up, he'd carefully carried her into his bedroom—only because she'd be more comfortable there and not because he wanted the chance to see her in his bed.

After covering her with a blanket and taking a minute to watch her settle beneath the covers as easily as she'd settled into his heart, he'd gone to check on Timmy. He'd smiled as he made out the sleeping form of his son—arms and legs sprawled out in all directions, hogging the bed with Sam's old stuffed bear dangling from one hand over the edge of the mattress.

Sam had been told on more than one occasion that he hogged the bed. It had made for a no-harm, no-foul excuse as to why he preferred to sleep alone. But then again, he'd had more than a few go-to excuses over the years. Ways to get out of trouble with some fast words and easy smile.

He didn't need his father or his brothers to tell him there was no easy out this time. One way or the other, he was in for the long haul.

Pushing off the couch, Sam took a minute to stretch out the kinks in his neck and back before heading down the hall and quietly opening his bedroom door. He sucked in a deep breath, arrested by the sight of Kara still asleep. She lay curled on her side facing him, her hands tucked beneath her cheek, her blond hair spread out across the navy pillow. Her lips parted on a soft sigh as her chest rose and fell, and he caught himself before he could echo the sound as he took in the delicate curves outlined by the thin sheets. He could have watched her for hours, but before that unsettling thought had time to take hold, he heard a sound from the other bedroom.

Not the gut-wrenching cries he'd heard the other night, but the soft call of his son's voice. "Sam?"

"Hey, Timmy," he said as he peered inside the room. "Everything okay?"

The little boy's hair was tousled from sleep, popping up in the same cowlicks and curls Sam had always hated as a kid. His green eyes were wide and curious as he looked around the room, but Sam gave a relieved sigh when he didn't see any tears. "I was sleeping, but then I woke up."

"Yeah, you spent the night, remember? Your Aunt Kara did, too."

"We played games and looked at the models when you were gone."

"You just looked at 'em, huh?" Sam asked, seeing that the models were still in their wrapped boxes and feeling a bit of disappointment. He'd really thought that with Timmy's love of puzzles he might be as into putting the cars together as he'd been as a kid. That it might be something they'd have in common.

"Uh-huh. Aunt Kara wanted to put them together, but that's our job 'cause we're mechanics."

"So you wanted to wait for me?"

Timmy nodded. "I tried to stay awake for you to come home, but you were gone a long time."

"My sister wasn't feeling good, so I wanted to go see her. But I'm sorry I wasn't here to play with you last night," he said as he sat down on the bed beside his son.

"That's okay. Aunt Kara played with me but—"

"But what?"

"I think she was sad."

Sam didn't doubt Kara had smiled for her nephew and tried her hardest to keep her emotions from showing through, but he wasn't surprised Timmy had sensed the sorrow she'd been trying to hide. "We all have days when we just feel sad."

"Uh-huh," the boy agreed, resting his head against Sam's side. It felt like the most natural thing in the world to put his arm around his son's shoulders and hold him close. "But when you're here, that makes her happy."

"You think so?"

"Like at the beach… Aunt Kara was laughing when you tackled her, but she didn't even have the football," he added with disgust filling his voice.

Sam couldn't help grinning. His son—the gridiron expert. "That was funny, wasn't it?"

Sam knew fatherhood wasn't always going to be a day at the beach, but wasn't there something to be said for having fun together, for knowing how to make his son happy? To make the woman he—loved?—happy…

A hell of a lot, he decided, certainty pouring through his veins as he thought about spending the rest of his life doing just that. And when times were tough, he still wanted to be there, the way Jake had been at Sophia's side last night. The way Sam wished he could have been at Kara's side when Ella was born all those years ago.

He couldn't change the past, but he definitely wanted Kara to be part of his future.

Hopping off the bed, Timmy checked out the shelf across the room. "What's this?" he asked, pulling out a baseball glove so old and worn that some of the laces were broken and the leather was cracked in places.

"That's a baseball glove my dad used when he was a kid. He gave it to me when I was a little boy." Timmy stuck his right hand inside, the glove comically large on the end of his arm. Moving the glove to the correct hand, Sam added, "Now I'd like to give it to you."

"To me?" Timmy's eyes widened, and Sam was taken back to the evening before when Timmy had asked if he had a little boy.

God, it had been so hard not to blurt out the truth then and there. But Timmy wasn't ready for that…or was he? Sam saw a longing in his son's eyes that had nothing to do with a raggedy glove. Going with his gut—or maybe it was with his heart—he said, "Do you remember when you asked if I had a little boy?" At Timmy's nod, he added, "The truth is, I'd really like you to be my little boy."

Timmy frowned, and Sam could practically see the wheels turning in his head. He was smart, no question about that, but he was still only four years old. Was Sam pushing too hard, too fast? Remembering the boy's reaction following the nightmare, he braced for another rejection.

"You mean—you'd be my daddy?"

"Yeah, if that's okay with you."

Unfiltered astonishment lit Timmy's features and grabbed hold of Sam's heart. "I've never had a daddy before." His face fell a little, and Sam wondered if Timmy was thinking of his mother. But then hope brightened his gaze again. "If you're gonna be my dad, maybe—maybe Aunt Kara can be my mom, and we can all be a family!"

Chapter Thirteen

Kara's eyelids fluttered open as she jerked awake. She blinked against the bright light streaming though the room, her eyes feeling grainy and dry. She pushed into a sitting position, startled to realize she was in Sam's king-sized bed…alone. Had he carried her there? It was the only explanation, and yet the last thing she remembered was Sam pulling her into his arms after she told him about Ella.

It had been so long since she'd told anyone the whole story….

Reaching up, she touched the locket holding her daughter's picture, but the pain of reopening old wounds wasn't as sharp as usual.

After a quick trip to the hall to the bathroom where she did her best to smooth her hair and wash away the dark smudges that were all that remained of her mascara, she followed the sound of voices and stopped just outside the kitchen doorway.

"Oh, nice shot!" Sam cheered after his son tossed a small *O*-shaped piece of cereal across the table and into his mouth. Sam returned the favor only to have the cereal bounce off a giggling Timmy's chin and onto the floor.

"You missed."

Sam laughed. "Okay, let's try again."

This shot, too, was off the mark, hitting the little boy in the forehead and sending him sprawling back in his chair like he'd been seriously wounded. "Missed again!"

"I'm starting to think you're missing the point of actually catching the cereal," Sam argued. Even with his back to her, Kara could hear the smile in his voice, the relaxed way he was talking to the little boy.

"You know, we are going to have some mess to clean up before your aunt wakes up."

"If we had a dog, the floor'd already be clean."

"A dog, huh?"

"Uh-huh."

"Do you have a dog back in San Diego?"

"No. Mommy said you can't have a dog in an apartment 'cause it needs a yard to play and poop in."

Sam choked back a laugh. "Well, that's true enough, I suppose. But you know what? My brother Nick's girlfriend, Darcy, has a dog that had puppies not too long ago. She and Nick want to find good homes for them."

"Really?"

"Really." He cleared his throat. "Of course that would mean we'd need to find a house with a yard big enough for a doghouse and maybe a tree house for you. Uncle Drew builds houses for a living and he's shown me a few things about building."

"Could I help, too?"

"Would you like that? To help me build a doghouse for the puppy and a tree house for you?"

A home for the two of them… Kara knew that was what Sam was really trying to build.

What was it that Olivia had said? That Timmy didn't have to choose between her and Sam? That he could love them both? That might be true, but he couldn't live with them both.

If she moved to Clearville, she could see Timmy whenever she wanted. She didn't doubt for a moment that Sam would let her be a part of the boy's life. But even then, it would only be a small part. She'd be back to fulfilling her role as his aunt, the only role she'd known when Marti was alive.

But things had changed since her sister's death. Kara would never think of taking her sister's place in Timmy's life, but in her heart—oh, in her heart she'd already come to think of him as her son. As the boy she would raise. She wanted to be there when he woke up and tuck him into bed at night.

She couldn't do that as his aunt.

As his aunt, she'd wake up alone, go to bed alone, sleep alone…

"Hey, you're awake."

She jumped at the sound of Sam's voice as he caught sight of her lurking in the doorway. His concerned gaze searched hers as he stepped close enough for her to feel the heat from his body. "How are you feeling? Did you sleep okay?"

Kara nodded, feeling a slight kink in her neck. "I must have since I fell asleep on the couch but woke up in your bed."

Sam's grin was unrepentant as he slid his hands beneath her hair. "I couldn't leave you on the couch. It's nowhere near as comfortable as stretching out on a bed."

Had his voice lowered on that last word or was it only

her imagination, fueled by the feeling of his thumbs pressing into her flesh, that had her thinking of the two of them lying on a mattress with him touching more than the back of her neck? "I, um—oh!"

He touched on a particularly sensitive spot, and she held back a moan as she turned to putty in his hands.

"How does that feel?"

Amazing…arousing…addicting…and that was only the beginning of the alphabet. She could have gone through the rest of the letters, describing how his touch made her feel in glorious detail. "Sam…"

"Hey, Aunt Kara!" Timmy called out. "Me and Sam—Me and Dad had cereal for breakfast."

Kara sucked in a breath as the little boy called Sam "Dad." Sam slid his hands from her neck to her shoulders as if bracing her for the emotional blow she'd just taken. "You told him," she whispered around the ache in her throat.

"We had a bit of a breakthrough," he explained, his voice hoarse with his own emotions. "One I'd like to discuss with you."

The intensity in his expression was underscored by a hint of uncertainty, but she already knew what he was going to say. Sam was ready for the two of them to move forward with their lives here in Clearville. A life that included a home with a yard, a tree house and a dog, but didn't include her.

Tears welled in her eyes and she blinked furiously as Sam turned away to talk to his son. "Hey, Tim, why don't you go get started on that first model? Be careful when you open the box. There's gonna be a lot of little pieces to put together."

Timmy pushed away from the table with an excited cry. He followed Sam's reminder to put his dishes in the sink, where they landed with a loud clatter, before he headed down the hall to his room.

"You told him," she repeated, trying to keep the accusation from her tone and not entirely sure she'd succeeded.

Sam shook his head. "Not exactly."

"He's calling you 'Dad.'"

"Yeah." Sam ducked his head as if trying to hide how much hearing his son call him that meant to him. After explaining the conversation the two of them had had in the bedroom, he added, "I'm not sure if Timmy really understands that I am his father or if he's just getting a kick out of calling me that."

"Whether he understands or not isn't really important, is it? What matters is that he wants you to be his dad."

"He wants more than that, Kara." He slid his palms down her arms and linked their fingers together. He squeezed her hand, his touch thawing the numbness that had seeped through her. "He wants you to be a part of his life, too."

A part…right. The beloved aunt who would come and visit on vacations and holidays.

"I want more than that, Sam," she interrupted.

"More?" Surprise and something else flickered in his eyes, but Kara couldn't stop to wonder about it. Couldn't stop to think or she'd lose her nerve.

"After we went to the beach, Timmy said it was like having a 'real' family—with a daddy, a mommy and a little boy."

"Kara—"

"No, just let me say this, please." Her emotions were bouncing around inside her like the balls in some kind of out-of-control lottery drawing, but she shoved them aside. She had to be calm about this, reasonable, to convince Sam that this idea—as crazy and illogical as it was—made sense.

"You told me once that you wished Timmy could have a childhood like your own, with two parents raising him under one roof. He can still have that childhood. *We* can give that to him, Sam. I know you're glad he's accepted you as his father, but Timmy was raised by a single mom. He's used to having a woman in his life. And then there's school."

Kara knew she was babbling but couldn't make the words stop as she spelled out how she could keep up the type of program Timmy's preschool had offered. "I know I'm not his mother, Sam, but I love him. I love him so much and—"

I love you. The words were on the tip of her tongue, but they froze there as twelve years disappeared and suddenly she was eighteen again—pregnant, afraid and desperately in love. She'd poured her heart out to Curtis, telling him about the baby, about the life she saw for the three of them, about the future they could have. She'd told him how much she loved him and practically begged him to say the words in return. But he hadn't. He'd just stared at her in silence.... Exactly as Sam was doing now, she thought, as she caught sight of the look on his face. She didn't think he would look more stunned if she told him she was taking Timmy to live on the moon.

The echo of her voice filled the room, and Kara crossed her arms over her stomach. She'd made a huge mistake. Why had she thought Sam would agree to such a ridiculous idea? Just because she wanted so desperately to be included in Timmy's life, to be included in Sam's, didn't mean Sam wanted the same thing. He didn't need her. He didn't love her...

Finally, the sound of Sam's cell phone broke through the fallout her words left behind. He reached out toward the counter, fumbling to pick it up, his actions like those of someone swatting at the snooze button after the alarm jarred them from a deep sleep.

"Yeah, hello?" He listened for a moment, some of the stunned disbelief clearing from his features. "That's great, Mom." Lowering the mouthpiece, he told Kara, "They're releasing Sophia from the hospital."

He was silent for another few seconds, his inscrutable gaze focused on Kara with such intensity, she couldn't look away, couldn't blink, couldn't breathe… "That's really good news. Give Sophia a hug for me, will you? Oh, and I've got some news of my own. Kara and I are getting married."

"Congratulations, sweetheart! Welcome to our family!"

Kara's step faltered slightly as Vanessa Pirelli's voice carried across the lush backyard. Sam told her his family was putting together an impromptu engagement party, but she hadn't expected this. Pink linens covered the picnic tables in the yard. Matching balloons swayed in the breeze and tiny white lights sparkled in the surrounding trees. Music and laughter filled the early evening air.

After the way the Pirellis had embraced Timmy, she shouldn't have been surprised. But the warm welcome and the party they'd put together on such short notice brought tears to her eyes.

"Too late to back out," Sam murmured at her side, placing his hand at her hip. "My mother's claimed you as one of her own now."

Kara shivered as the warmth of his touch seeped through the lightweight fabric of her dress. Was it her imagination or did the heated look in his eyes mean he wanted to do some claiming of his own? She wished she could be sure. Wished she knew what Sam was thinking.

In the two days since her proposal, she and Sam had had plenty of time to talk. They'd talked about the call she placed to the college, informing them she wouldn't be back to teach in the fall. They'd talked about Olivia's eardrum-splitting reaction and her offer to help coordinate moving Kara's things in exchange for being maid of honor. They'd talked about looking for a house and finding a preschool for Timmy.

But they hadn't talked about what marriage would mean for the two of them—only about what it would mean for the *three* of them. The chance to live as a family together under one roof as two parents and one child.

But as husband and wife? That complicated subject hadn't come up.

"Wow," Timmy breathed. "Look at all the balloons. Is it your birthday?"

Sam laughed as he tousled his son's curls. "Still not my birthday, bud. But why don't you go see if there's any cake?"

"There is," the boy said knowingly.

"What makes you so sure?"

Pointing across the crowded lawn, he said, "That's the baker lady."

Following his small finger, Kara spotted Debbie Mattson talking to Vince Pirelli. The pretty blonde was only one of Sam's many friends gathered in the backyard. Kara recognized a few other faces, as well, people she'd met over the past few days who would now be her neighbors and hopefully her friends.

Holding out her arms to greet them, Vanessa's warm smile and encompassing hug brought tears to Kara's eyes. If Sam's mother had any doubts about the suddenness of their engagement, she didn't let it show. "I'm so happy for both of you! All of you!"

"Thank you so much for this, Vanessa. It's amazing."

"It's the least we can do since your own family is so

far away. What do your parents think of your whirlwind romance?"

Kara wondered if her laugh sounded as fake to Vanessa and Sam as it did to her own ears. "Unfortunately, I haven't had a chance to talk to them yet. They're both at a medical seminar. This isn't the kind of announcement you want to make over voice mail, so we've been playing phone tag." She smiled, even though words weren't entirely true.

If she and her parents were playing a game, it was more like keep-away. She kept tossing messages in their direction, but so far neither Marcus nor Kathryn Starling had returned them. Kara would just as soon put the conversation off as long as possible. She knew they wouldn't be happy with her decision. Wouldn't be happy, period. And she wanted to be happy.

As Vanessa led them over to a table loaded with finger food and drinks, Kara glanced at Sam. Her stomach did a slow somersault that would have done her nephew proud as he caught her eye. She wanted *them* to be happy. The three of them together as a family and the two of them as a couple. She wanted to be Timmy's mother, to stand by his side and watch him grow, but only as much as she wanted to be Sam's wife, to stand by his side and grow old together.

I love you.

Sam stopped, and for a second, so did Kara's heart as she feared she'd said the words out loud.

Three small, simple words, powerful enough to change her world.

But the last time she'd spoken those words, they'd signaled the end of a relationship, not the beginning, and the courage she'd found to ask Sam to marry her failed her entirely when it came to telling him how she felt.

"You'll want to decide on a date soon," Vanessa was saying. "Clearville only has a few locations large enough for a reception. Unless you want to have it here like Sophia and Jake did. That was such a wonderful day..." Her voice trailed off as she got lost in the memories of her only daughter's wedding before refocusing with a smile on her eldest son and his fiancée. "Nick and Darcy have already booked their location at Hillcrest. It's a gorgeous Victorian hotel just outside of town and the grounds are lovely. Of course, it's not a very large venue...."

"I don't have any family," Darcy said in an aside to Kara as Vanessa went on. "So we're perfectly happy with a small wedding."

"Small sounds good," she murmured back, and as for family, Kara wondered if her parents would even attend.

"Don't you both think so?" Vanessa finished as she glanced back and forth between Kara and Sam.

"That all sounds great, Mom," Sam answered, and Kara could only hope he'd been paying more attention than she had.

"Where's the ring?" Sophia stepped forward, her hands folded below the swell of her belly. "An engagement isn't really official without a ring, is it?"

Unlike the rest of the Pirelli family, Sam's sister had held back during the welcoming hugs. Not that Kara could blame the other woman. After all, Sophia was also the only member of Sam's family to know Kara hadn't been up front with Sam from the start. She had every reason to have her doubts and suspicions.

Clenching her ringless fingers in front of her, Kara prayed Sophia wouldn't pick this moment to air all those suspicions. "This has been sudden," she admitted with a glance at Sam. "We really haven't had time..."

At her side, Sam shifted his weight from one foot to the other and heaved a sigh. "You had to go and blow this, didn't you, Sophia?"

His sister blinked, clearly surprised at being called out in front of everyone. "Sam—"

"I wanted to do this my way, but since you insist." Reaching into his pocket, he pulled out a small black box.

A sudden gasp caught in the throat of every woman within sight, but Kara couldn't pull enough air into her lungs to make a sound. Lifting her hand, Sam placed the box on her palm. "The jeweler told me you could exchange it if you like, but when I saw this, I immediately thought of you."

Her hands shook as she opened the box. A gorgeous round diamond surrounded by white gold filigree gleamed against the dark velvet. The antique-style setting was traditional and yet different from a typical solitaire. "Oh, Sam, it's beautiful."

Sam slipped the ring from the box, his gaze so sincere, so compelling, Kara couldn't bring herself to look away. Her heart started pounding as he knelt down in front of her. "I know we can't go back in time, but maybe you could pretend this is the first time I asked you…" His smile might have been a little wry, but his green eyes glowed with an emotion Kara was afraid to name. "Kara, will you marry me?"

"Yes," she whispered, her voice shaking. "Yes, Sam, I'll marry you."

There'd been a time in Sam's life when, no matter how hard he studied, the second a test was placed in front of him, all the answers flew out the window. He'd stare at the questions and freeze—unable to think, to move. Sometimes it felt like he'd been unable to breathe. That same paralyzing fear had held him in its grip as he'd waited for Kara's response.

He *knew* the answer. Hell, she'd been the one to bring

up the idea of getting married in the first place. But her soft words washed over him like magic, setting him free. Breath rushed back into his lungs and his pulse pounded a wild rhythm he couldn't control…any more than he could control the desire to kiss her.

Surging to his feet, Sam caught Kara around the waist, pulling her body to his. She made a soft sound, one that combined surrender and hunger, as he claimed her mouth with his. He buried his hands in her silky hair, sifting his fingers through the soft strands and tilting her head to deepen the kiss. He held her tightly enough to feel her heart pounding against his and he wanted more….

"Geez, Sam, get a room." Drew's laughter broke the moment, but as he slapped a hand on Sam's shoulder, he gave him a what-the-hell look far too familiar from the wild days of his youth.

Sam sucked in the cool night air. He'd gone too far. Hell, he knew Kara wasn't the type for public displays but he'd wanted to prove—what? How much he wanted his fiancée? How easily Kara could turn him inside out with nothing more than a look?

But when he glanced down at the woman in question, Kara appeared as stunned as he felt by the kiss. Her breasts rose on an uneven breath, and her eyes shimmered with an almost smoky cast.

Sam cleared his throat. "Speaking of rooms…" Her jaw dropped slightly, her lips parting on an unspoken thought, and he was tempted to push, to tease her a little. "I know you're not comfortable moving in together until after the wedding."

Kara ducked her head, a touch of pink highlighting her cheeks. The shy response was a contrast to the passionate response to his kiss, and Sam was glad he hadn't made a joke.

"This is a small town, and people will talk…"

Her voice trailed away at the end, making Sam wonder what she might have already heard. He longed to say he didn't give a damn about gossip, but that would have been the old Sam talking. The one who wasn't a father with a young son, the carefree bachelor without a fiancée's feelings to consider.

Maybe waiting until after the wedding to move in together *was* old-fashioned, but under the circumstances, it felt right.

What didn't feel right was Kara staying in a hotel room. A situation that felt far too…temporary. A packed bag, an early-morning check out, and Kara could be gone before he knew it.

Forcing the doubt aside, he said, "I thought we could go look at houses in the morning."

"Hmm, one with a big yard for a tree house and a dog?"

Sam gave a short laugh, remembering the list of requirements he and Timmy had discussed. "You heard that part, huh?"

"I did. He's so excited."

Yeah, his son didn't leave much in question when it came to how he felt about his dad and Aunt Kara getting married or about the three of them living together. He'd even come up with the idea before Kara had.

If you're gonna be my dad, maybe—maybe Aunt Kara can be my mom, and we can all be a family! Pretty cut-and-dry. Not all that different from Kara's proposal, but a world away from the one Sam had wanted to make.

He hadn't had a ring at the time, but he'd already known the words he wanted to say. *I love you, Kara. I want to spend the rest of my life with you. I used to think loving someone was a responsibility, a burden, but now I know it's a gift. The second amazing gift you've given me. First you gave me the son I never knew I had, and now, if you say yes, you'll be giving me the wife I never dreamed I'd find.*

Now Kara was wearing his ring, but his proposal was still locked up tight. He wasn't sure if the words were ones she wanted to hear. Not when they were getting married because it made sense and Timmy needed a woman in his life. And not when they had yet to set a date.

Sam understood Kara wanting to tell her parents first, but the Starlings had seemed almost impossible to reach. An hour after surprising his mother with their announcement, the old-fashioned Clearville grapevine had spread the news of their engagement throughout town. Yet, with all the technology at Kara's disposal—phones, Facebook, email—he had to wonder about her inability to reach her parents.

Could it be she wasn't trying that hard because she was afraid of what they might say? Something along the lines of how a small-town mechanic with a mere high school diploma wasn't good enough for her and how she could do so much better…?

"Sam?" Kara tilted her head, a worried frown pulling at her eyebrows. "Is everything okay?"

"Yeah. It's fine."

He'd meant what he said when he told Kara Timmy deserved to have two parents living under the same roof. If he'd have married Marti it would have been to fulfill his sense of duty, of responsibility. He never would have expected her love.

But with Kara…He didn't expect her love. He craved it like the air he breathed. Sam didn't know if there was any chance that Kara's feelings for him might one day grow into something more, but even if he wasn't a man she could love, he would be a man she could respect. He would keep his word even if it killed him.

* * *

Later in the evening, Sam spotted his sister sitting on the front porch swing and walked over to join her. Sophia had one foot tucked beneath her and used the other to rock the swing at an easy pace. "Where's your watchdog?"

Sophia rolled her eyes, but it wasn't enough to disguise the love she clearly felt for her husband. "I made the mistake of asking for some juice. He's probably out raiding an organic citrus grove for a bunch of oranges to squeeze with his own hands."

"He's a good guy."

"The best. Kind of like my brothers," she said, bumping him with her shoulder. "You're a great guy, Sam, and I have to admit this whole engagement has me worried. How can you trust Kara after the way she kept Timmy a secret from you?"

"I know how bad it looked, but Kara would have told me the truth. All she's ever wanted was to do what's best for Timmy."

"And that's the problem."

"What do you mean?"

"Kara wants to do the right thing for Timmy, but what about doing the right thing for you?" Sophia sighed, her gaze growing distant as she stared out at the fading sorbet colors of the sunset. "I keep thinking about what my life would have been like if Todd had 'done the right thing.'"

Sam cleared his throat to disguise his total aversion to the thought. Todd Dunworthy was the son of the rich family Sophia had worked for as a maid during her years in Chicago. The selfish SOB had been engaged while seeing Sophia on the side and had dropped Sam's sister the moment he'd found out she was carrying his child. "You don't, um, wish that he had…"

"What? Geez, Sam!" Reaching out, she backhanded him on the arm. "No!"

He flinched as he ducked away. "Well—geez yourself, Fifi!" he shot back, using her childhood nickname. "What'd you expect me to think when you go and say something like that?"

"I *love* Jake. That's what you're supposed to know, no matter what!" With a huff of breath, she settled back against the swing and said, "And that's my point. If I had married Todd because I got pregnant, I would never have met Jake. We never would have had the chance to fall in love. I wouldn't have known what it felt like to know someone so completely and love them with my whole heart. I would have missed that." She pinned him with a knowing look that made her seem far too wise to be his little sister. "It breaks my heart to think *you* might miss feeling the same way about someone."

A weight pressed on Sam's chest, and he released a heavy sigh.

To know someone so completely and love them with my whole heart.

His gaze locked in on Kara like a homing beacon. She was laughing at something his father said, the sound drifting across the yard to tease his skin on the summer breeze. The setting sun created a golden aura around her blond hair, and she was so beautiful, it almost hurt to look at her.

"You don't have to worry about that, Sophia," he murmured.

He knew exactly what it felt like to love a woman the way his sister described. But to have the woman he loved love him as strongly in return?

That was something his sister could worry about.

Chapter Fourteen

"It was sweet of Maddie to ask if Timmy could spend the night," Kara said, as she and Sam drove back toward town. The nerves that had first plagued her disappeared as the night went on, and she'd ended up having a great time with Sam's family and friends.

She'd felt relaxed and happy and welcomed, as if she'd been part of the small community her whole life. As if she'd been a part of Sam's family her whole life.

"Don't get me wrong, Maddie likes Timmy, but my niece is a big-picture kind of girl."

"What do you mean?"

"I think she's trying to show Nick and Darcy what a great older sis she'd be. She's angling for a baby brother or—" Sam cut off his own words, and even in the faint glow of the shifting streetlights, Kara could see the regret written across the lines on his forehead.

Reaching out, she covered his hand with hers. "It's all

right, Sam. I promise I won't fall apart every time someone mentions having a baby."

"No, I know you won't." Turning his wrist, he linked their fingers together and gave a gentle squeeze. "You're far too strong for that."

Kara shook her head. "I'm not strong."

"You survived a heartbreaking loss when you were only twenty years old."

"Eighteen," she correctly softly. "I skipped a few grades in school."

"See? Smart and strong."

"If I'd been stronger, I would have stuck with my plans to teach kindergarten." She'd given up on that dream long ago, but having Timmy in her life on a daily basis reminded her more and more of her old desire to open children's eyes to their own hopes and dreams and futures where the possibility existed for them to do anything, to be anything....

"Don't be so hard on yourself. After what you went through, no one would blame you for feeling that way or changing your plans."

"I know," she whispered, "but that was a long time ago."

Maybe she was ready to try again.

To be a kindergarten teacher—or to be a mother?

The thought came out of nowhere, but what had once been an impossibility now no longer seemed so unthinkable. After losing Ella, the pain and emptiness inside was so great, she'd sworn she would never take that risk again.

To lose another child...

Reaching up, Kara touched the locket around her neck. Her love for Ella was still strong, still *alive* after all this time. She hadn't lost that at all. And even though she'd only had her daughter for a short time, Kara realized she wouldn't give those few, precious days up for anything.

Taking a deep breath, she asked, "What do Nick and Darcy think of Maddie's plan?"

"Darcy seems intrigued, but Nick's about to have a heart attack. He swore he'd never get married again, so I'm sure he thought Maddie would always be an only child."

What about Timmy? Kara wanted to ask. *Would he always be an only child?*

But the very idea of having another child was still so new, so tender, she needed to let it grow, sheltered in her own mind, before exposing it to the world. And even though Timmy was already four, Sam was still very much a new father. Maybe he, like Nick, wouldn't be ready to even think of having another child.

And of course, there was more to having a child than simply thinking about it. Things like sex. A small shiver raced through Kara. She already knew what it was like to be kissed by Sam. To feel his lips move against her own. To taste his passion…and his control. Maybe it had to do with being mechanically inclined, but he seemed to know exactly how to speed things up and when to slow down. Not to mention all the buttons to push to turn her on.

But it was hard for Kara to think in terms of doing the same for him. She knew he had far more experience with the opposite sex than she had, that he'd been with women who were far more beautiful, far more exciting. Women like…her sister.

Sam had admitted his relationship with Marti was little more than a fling, but Marti had always had such confidence when it came to men. A confidence Kara had lacked in all of her relationships. Could she really expect that with Sam it would be any different?

It is *different. Sam is different.*

She trusted Sam. She trusted him with Timmy. She

trusted him with her few precious memories of Ella. She could trust him with her heart.

"So, tell me about this house we're going to look at tomorrow," Kara said over her shoulder as she circled the small counter dividing the living area from the small kitchenette.

Was it his imagination or was she nervous? She'd been quiet on the ride back to the hotel, but Sam had blamed that on his stupid mistake in bringing up Maddie's desire for a younger sibling. Looking at Kara now, though, he didn't see any signs of sorrow on her lovely face. But between the quick glances she was shooting his way and the four feet of counter space she'd used to separate the two of them, he knew something was up.

Was it because of the kiss? Thanks to his lack of control earlier, did she think he was going to attack her now that they were alone?

Resisting the urge to swear, he focused on Kara's question instead and filled her in on the details of the house. "Technically, it belongs to Drew. When he's not working on a custom house for a client, he'll work on remodels to keep busy. Once the remodeling's done, he sells the house to a buyer who's looking for a walk-in-ready home. He had a couple interested in the place, but their loan fell through."

"It sounds great. Timmy's so excited about the tree house, the dog, everything."

"Yeah, he is," Sam said with enough emphasis to make Kara pause.

"Is everything okay?"

"Maybe you can tell me."

"Me?"

"Yes, *you* Kara. Maybe you can tell me what you're thinking, what you're feeling."

"About looking for a house? I told you, I think it's great and Timmy—"

"Will love it." A muscle flexed in his jaw, and he felt as if he were forcing the words out. "You're giving up so much—your friends, your family, your home, your career. Is it all for Timmy? Is any of this about *you?* About what you want? Is any of it about *us?*"

Kara's eyes widened at the rough demand. "I'm not giving up anything, Sam," she whispered. "I'm getting everything I've ever wanted."

"Yeah," he agreed hoarsely. "Timmy."

"Yes. And you." With her gaze locked on his, she circled the counter and erased the distance between them. She didn't stop until the silky material of her skirt brushed against his thighs. Reaching up, she cupped his face in her hands. He could feel the faint tremor in her fingers against his jaw, but her words were steady as she said, "I want you to be my friend, my family, my home. I want you to be my husband. I want you. All of you."

Something broke loose inside of Sam at her words. The control—or was it the fear?—holding him back snapped, and he pulled Kara into his arms. His mouth captured hers in a hungry kiss, so unlike the others they'd shared, so unlike any kiss he'd given or received…ever. He wanted to lose himself just for a short while in a place where only the two of them existed. And then it happened. The outside world fell away, leaving only heat and softness as her mouth opened beneath his. He traced the fullness of her lips with his tongue before plunging inside.

A small sound escaped her, and for a moment, Sam worried he'd pushed too hard, taken too much, too soon. But then her tongue circled his, pulling him deeper. For possibly the first time, he realized he wasn't taking. He was giving, and Kara was accepting everything he had and offering herself back in return.

And it still wasn't enough. Sam slid one hand down Kara's back while he buried the other in her hair. It flowed like warm silk through his fingers. He cupped the back of her head to hold her still, even as his palm grasped her bottom to urge her closer. He pressed her tight to his arousal, letting her feel the effect she had on him, and groaned when she arched even closer.

Sam broke the kiss, filling his starving lungs with air and his starving soul with the knowledge that he'd fallen in love. He hadn't expected to find someone like Kara in his small hometown. He hadn't expected to find her at all. She was like no one he'd ever met before. So strong and yet so vulnerable. So caring and yet so fiercely protective. So beautiful, inside and out.

He skimmed his lips across her cheek to the curve of her jaw. Kara rolled her head to the side, offering full access to her throat. His kiss followed the enticing V-neck of the pale pink dress as it dipped between her breasts.

Kara felt his breath bathing her skin, and her heart seemed to melt in the heat, pooling low in her belly without skipping a single, pulsating beat. Her nipples tightened even though he hadn't touched her. But she wanted him to. Oh, how she wanted him to!

"Sam." She murmured his name in a throaty whisper, and he answered, lifting her into his arms and carrying her into the bedroom. Her dress slid away with the whisper of a zipper and the soft swish of material. Her bra and panties followed, disappearing into the room's darkened corners. The light in Sam's eyes as he looked at her banished the monsters of self-doubt, and she didn't have to worry about not being pretty enough, sexy enough, shapely enough.

"You are so beautiful," he whispered roughly, and she believed him.

He lowered her onto the silky softness of the bed and followed her down, but when she tried to touch him, tried to tug the shirt from his shoulders, he caught her hands in his. "My turn," he murmured against her lips, and Kara remembered the night on the couch. The night when he'd let her touch and taste and feel…

He molded her curves to his every kiss, every caress, until she couldn't take any more. Until all she wanted was more. She teetered on the edge of a promised pleasure so profound, Kara already knew she would never be the same again, but she waited. Caught on the brink until Sam took them both over the edge. And when she landed back in the real world with the softness of the mattress beneath her and the hard strength of his body above her, she knew without a doubt that she'd fallen in love.

The ring of her cell phone jarred Kara from sleep. She squinted against the bright light filling the hotel room as two facts filtered through her fuzzy brain. She was naked and she was alone. Unease shifted through her stomach until she spotted the note on the bedside table next to her phone.

You looked like Sleeping Beauty, but I wouldn't have been able to stop at just one kiss.

Relief slipped out on a sigh until her phone rang a second time and she caught sight of her parents' number on the screen. Kara swallowed. This was not a conversation she wanted to have with her parents naked. But she'd only be delaying the inevitable and who knew when they might call back? Tucking the sheet beneath her breasts, she answered the call.

"Honestly, Kara, you've left a good dozen messages

over the past two days," her mother said by way of greeting before she could even say hello.

"Yes, well, I wanted to talk to you and Dad." Something most parents would have figured out by, oh, say the fourth or fifth message.

"Whatever it is, you have our attention. But only for the next fifteen minutes. We've both have speeches scheduled to start at ten."

"Right. Thanks for squeezing me in," Kara said, more relieved than annoyed. As painful as the next few minutes might be, at least they would be over quickly. "I'm getting married."

There. That didn't even use up fifteen seconds. Her parents would have plenty of time for coffee before heading to the auditorium.

"You're what?"

"I'm staying here in Clearville and getting married."

Her father reacted to the news as predicted, bringing up her job, her chance to be chair of the department. "You're throwing away years of hard work and for what?"

"I don't know, Dad. The chance to be happy?"

"Happy." He echoed the word as if it had no meaning. "Doing what?"

"Doing what I've always wanted to do. Raising a family. Being a mother." And maybe in a year or two, when Timmy was going to school all day, she'd look into going back to the classroom, too. Not as a teacher, but as a student. She wanted to go back to school and take the required classes needed for elementary education. She was ready now to fulfill her dream of teaching kindergarten.

"Kara, you're a college professor." He stressed the words, making them sound so much bigger, so much more important than the ones she'd used. As if being a wife and mother was something any woman could do and not something she should waste her talents and intelligence pursuing.

"This is what I want. If you can't be happy for me, then at least...be quiet."

Her words, even softly spoken, were as close as she'd come to talking back in nearly two decades, and a stunned silence sounded in response before her mother's voice came across the line. "Kara, I know how hard Marti's death was on you. On all of us. But this rush into a marriage...are you sure you aren't reacting out of grief?"

"I'm not, Mom. Really. I won't pretend I wasn't devastated by Marti's death or that I don't miss her every day, but this isn't a reaction. It's what I want."

"All right then, if that's true, fine. But why not come back home, finish out this semester. Then in five or six months, if you still feel so strongly, you can move back and go from there."

As much as Kara hated to admit it, her mother's words chipped away at her confidence. Her father's sledgehammer blows she could withstand, but her mother was like an ice pick—pointed, sharp and precise. *Was* she rushing things with Sam? He'd asked about all she was giving up to move to Clearville, but what about the sacrifice *he* was making? After all, he was the one who'd enjoyed a bachelor's lifestyle while she'd barely gone on a handful of dates in the past few years. In time, would Sam regret giving up his freedom?

Hating the cracks inching their way beneath the surface, Kara said her goodbyes to her parents as quickly as she could. She needed to go see Sam. One smile, one kiss, and he'd wipe away all her doubts.

"Hey, um, you got a minute, Sam?"

Sam looked up to see Will lurking in the doorway to his

office and wondered with a touch of embarrassment how long the kid had been standing there. It might have been only a few seconds or it could have inched into five or ten minutes. He couldn't say for sure.

Time had lost meaning as he'd leisurely replayed every moment from the previous night. He had to be crazy to leave Kara to come into work, but he'd already been away from the garage too much. He did have a business to run, although if he didn't get his mind off the woman he loved, he could well end up running it into the ground.

It wasn't a thought that should make him smile, but he couldn't seem to keep the grin off his face.

"What's up, Will?"

"I was wondering…I mean, with all the time you've been spending with Timmy, I've been working here on my own this past week or so."

"You have, and if I haven't told you, I appreciate it. It's meant a lot to me to spend time with Tim, and I know the garage is in good hands even when I'm not around."

Will ducked his head but not before Sam saw the blush creeping up his neck. "Yeah, well, you're welcome. I'm glad to help out, and I figure with you and Kara getting married soon, that maybe you'll need even more help, you know. Like full-time help."

He had planned on hiring another part-time mechanic, but that had been when he still intended to hit every auction from the Northwest down to the South. Before he knew about Timmy and before he'd fallen in love with Kara.

Before he'd sold the Corvette to Billy Cummings.

Sam sighed over that, but only a little. Building a family meant more to him than fixing up a car ever could.

"That's great of you to offer, Will, but you've got school starting soon. It's your senior year. I don't want you missing out because you're here every night. Working on the weekends and a few afternoons during the week will be enough."

"No," Will muttered, his head downcast. "It won't."

"What do you mean?"

Lifting his chin, the teenager met Sam's gaze. "I need a full-time job. I'm dropping out of school."

Sam still had the conversation with Will on his mind when his phone rang a few minutes later.

"Sam Pirelli?"

"You got him," he said in response to the unfamiliar male voice on the other end of the line.

"This is Doctor Marcus Starling."

Doctor Marcus Starling…Kara's father. His soon-to-be father-in-law. Judging by the cool, almost impersonal greeting, Marcus Starling wouldn't be asking Sam to call him Dad anytime soon. He was pretty sure this call could only mean one thing. Kara had finally gotten hold of her parents to share the good news. "Hello, sir. It's good to finally talk to you."

"From what my daughter tells me, you and I have plenty to talk about."

Yeah, Sam could just imagine everything he and the heart surgeon would have in common. But he wasn't about to be intimidated by the other man. "I suppose we do. The first thing you should know is that I love your daughter. She's an amazing woman."

A brief hesitation on the other end of the line followed before Marcus questioned, "And Marti? I assume you must have found my younger daughter amazing, as well."

Sam gritted his teeth in an effort to hold back the words on the tip of his tongue. He deserved that. He might not like it, but he deserved it. And while he also didn't like much about the other man, he could sympathize for the loss his family had experienced. First Marti's death and now Kara's decision to move away with their only grandchild.

"Marti was a great girl, and I was sorry to hear about her death."

"And surprised to discover you're a father, I imagine."

"Timmy's a great kid, and I'm lucky to have him."

"And to have Kara, too? From the time Timmy was born, Kara was always there. Helping Marti when he was a baby any way she could. But the fact of the matter is that Timothy is not Kara's responsibility."

"You're right. He's not her responsibility at all. He's her nephew and she loves him."

"I'm not questioning Kara's love for Timothy. I'm questioning your love for Kara."

"Excuse me?"

"Have you thought of how much she's giving up to move there? She has a life here, a career she's worked hard to obtain. She's in line for head of the English department, and if she's named to the position, she'll be the youngest department chair at her college." At Sam's silence, Marcus asked, "She didn't tell you about that, did she? Kara has a bright future ahead of her. If you love her as much as you say you do, then you really should let her go."

When Kara stepped into the garage, she was surprised to hear the sound of a raised female voice coming from Sam's office. "I thought I could count on you to back me up on this, Sam!"

"All I'm saying is that it's Will's life and I think he's old enough and smart enough to make his own choices."

"He's smart enough to go to college, but only if he finishes high school!"

Kara stepped back as Nadine brushed by her on the way

out of the garage with a mumbled apology. "What was that about?" she asked as she stepped into the office.

Sam shot her a glance before refocusing on a stack of invoices on the desk. "Will wants to drop out of school to work here full-time."

"No wonder Nadine's upset. I know you think of Will as a friend and that you want to support him, but you can't encourage him to drop out of school. Education is too important."

"Having a roof over his head and food on the table is pretty important, too."

Kara blinked at the short response. He almost sounded angry at her, but why would he be when she was only trying to help? "If things are that bad, maybe there's another way to help out. Dropping out can't be the answer. Will has his whole future ahead of him. If he quits school to work full-time, he could—"

"He could what, Kara?" Sam pushed away from his chair and braced his hands on the desk. "End up a two-bit mechanic in a one-car town?"

Kara recoiled at the sting of sarcasm whipping through his words. "I would never say something like that. I never thought anything like that. I don't understand where this is coming from."

"Why didn't you tell me you were up for department chair at your college?"

That was the last thing she'd expected Sam to say, and she stared at him in surprise. "How did you even know about that?"

"Your father called me."

"My father? I can't believe he did that. He had no right—"

"What? He doesn't have the right to tell me the truth? Or do you think that I don't have the right to know the truth?"

Anger blazed in his eyes as he rounded the desk, coming to a stop inches away. "More Starling secrets, right? Anything else that you haven't told me?"

Only that she loved him.

But with the accusations he was throwing at her, Kara had no intention of telling him. Not when it would only be something he would twist around and use against her. "I didn't tell you about being up for chair because I didn't even know if I'd be named to the position. And what does it matter now that I've told the college I'm not coming back?"

"What matters is that you lied."

"I did not lie!"

"No. You just didn't bother to tell me."

"Like I didn't tell you about Timmy? That's what you're thinking, right, Sam? I told you how sorry I am, and I thought you'd forgiven me. But if you haven't…is this how it will always be? Are you going to keep throwing my mistakes back in my face? I can't live like that, Sam. I can't. I won't."

"Whoa, you look like hell."

Sam glared as his brother sank onto the stool beside him at the bar. The Clearville Bar and Grille had a good crowd, the patrons eager to start the weekend with an after-work happy hour. Sam wasn't sure why he'd agreed to meet Drew there considering he'd never felt less happy.

"I'm not sure this is good timing or bad, but as your best man, I wanted to talk about your bachelor party. Any chance that conversation would cheer you up?" Drew leaned back at the look Sam shot him. "I'm taking that as a no."

"Don't have to worry about a bachelor party if there's not going to be a wedding."

"Things are that bad?"

Yes. "No. Maybe. I don't know."

His expression sobering, Drew said, "If you're not sure about going through with this, now's the time to say so."

Sam stared hard at his brother. "Hell, Drew, who said I was the one who was unsure?"

At any other time, he might have been amused at catching his always-think-before-you-speak brother with his foot so firmly lodged in his mouth. "Sorry, I guess I just assumed. So Kara's getting cold feet?"

After filling his brother in on the conversation with Dr. Starling, he added, "Kara said the reason she didn't tell me she was up for department chair was because she wasn't planning on taking the position. Maybe that's the truth, I don't know. But that phone call blindsided me."

To know Kara had kept something so important from him reminded him too much of the way Heather had gone behind his back, applying for scholarships without telling him. Finding out about the promotion only reminded him that there was so much more out in the world for a woman like Kara than Clearville could offer. So much more than what he could offer. The thought of her leaving him behind was like a kick in the gut and he'd lashed out. But he had every right to be angry.

Are you going to keep throwing my mistakes back in my face? I can't live like that, Sam. I can't. I won't.

The memory of the hurt shimmering in Kara's brown eyes shook some of that certainty. He'd only had one conversation with *Doctor* Starling, but Sam could only imagine the man's reaction to his teenage daughter's pregnancy. How many times had he used Kara's "mistake" as a way to keep her in line?

Sam swore beneath his breath, tightening his hand around the cold beer bottle.

"So, in the interest of full disclosure, have you told Kara

everything? Have you told her you love her?" At Sam's answering silence, his brother shook his head. "Didn't think so."

He did love Kara. He loved how calm and cool she was on the outside and how kind and caring she was to anyone fortunate enough to see inside. He loved how fiercely proud and protective she was of his son. He loved when she let loose and laughed, and he understood why it wasn't always easy for her to do. That only made those moments seem like even more of a gift.

But the thought of telling a woman he loved her for the first time in over a decade had him so tied up in knots, he didn't know if he'd ever work his way free.

Almost as if knowing where his thoughts had gone, Drew said, "You know I never did ask you all those years ago, but when Heather left, why didn't you go with her?"

"Yeah, right," he scoffed. "They never would have let me in."

Drew raised his eyebrows. "To Oregon? Why? Is there some kind of statewide ban against you that I'm not aware of?"

Sam felt his face heat. "I thought you meant go with her to college," he muttered.

Heather had been as desperate to get into college as he'd been to get out of high school. Somehow their lives, which had once traveled so closely on the same path, had veered in different directions. He'd known once Heather was surrounded by other students as eager to learn and party and soak up the whole four-year experience, what they had wouldn't be enough to keep them together. And so when the time came, he'd let her go.

He'd taken the easy way out. Failing to try rather than trying and failing.

Not this time. Not with Kara. This was too important

for him to give up without giving his all. For the first time since the phone call with Kara's father, Sam felt a slight smile pull at his lips. Failure, as the saying went, was not an option.

"Hey, look! There's Dad's car." Timmy tugged on Kara's hand as they left Rolly's Diner and pointed down the narrow street.

Kara's stomach dipped at his excited words. She hadn't seen Sam since their fight earlier in the day, and she wasn't sure she was ready to see him now. Oh, why hadn't she ordered room service instead of going out for dinner? If they had, maybe Sam would have driven by and she'd have a little more time to nurse her wounds.

She'd really thought that he'd forgiven her for keeping Timmy a secret. She knew she'd made a mistake by not telling him the truth right away, but she'd apologized and she'd been completely honest since then.

Completely honest about everything except her feelings.

Her father never should have called Sam, but she couldn't help thinking that if she'd been truthful with Sam—about her feelings, about the stupid nomination for department chair—maybe he wouldn't have been so quick to jump to conclusions. Maybe he would have been more willing to listen to what she had to say.

Taking a deep breath, she looked in the direction her nephew pointed. A wave of disappointment washed over her. "Timmy, your dad's car is red, remember? That one's black."

A sleek, glossy black, nothing like the primer-spotted dull red of Sam's Corvette.

"He colored it," the little boy argued.

"You mean painted it?"

"Uh-huh."

Kara took a closer look at the car across the street and shook her head. "Sorry, Timmy, but that's not the same car. See? There's some other guy driving it."

The words were barely out of her mouth when Timmy pulled his hand from hers and raced down the sidewalk, hollering at the startled driver. "Hey, how come you got my dad's car?"

"Timmy!" Her heart in her throat, she caught the little boy by one arm before he reached the street. "What are you doing? You know better than to run off like that!"

Tears filled the little boy's eyes. "That man stole Dad's car. We gotta get it back!"

"Hey, is everything okay?"

Embarrassment heated Kara's cheeks as she realized Timmy's accusations had been loud enough to reach the "car thief."

"I'm really sorry—you're Billy, right?" she asked, recognizing the man as one of Sam's friends who'd attended their engagement party. "I'm sorry about this, but Timmy thinks you're driving Sam's car. I've tried to explain it's not his."

"Well, it's not Sam's car. At least it's not anymore."

"What do you mean?"

"He sold it to me a few days ago. Right after he finished the paint job."

"So you mean that is—was Sam's car?"

"Told you so," Timmy muttered at her side.

"But Sam said he was going to take the car to an auction." Where she knew he could have made far more money than by selling it to his friend. "Why would he sell it now?"

Billy shrugged. "I guess he found something that was worth more." Kara imagined she must have still looked completely stunned when he felt the need to add, "And I'm not talking about another car."

* * *

After Sam left the Bar and Grille, he'd wanted to go to the hotel to talk to Kara, to lay everything on the line and tell her how he felt, but Will had called with an emergency. A motorist was stranded on the highway outside of town, not far from the spot where Sam and Kara first met. As he pushed the tow truck over the speed limit, he hoped the breakdown was something simple, like a flat tire. He'd give a NASCAR pit crew a run for their money when it came to how fast he'd have that tire changed out, so he could be on his way back to town. Back to Kara.

The sun was sinking behind the mountains as he followed the bend in the road and spotted the vehicle up ahead—a blue minivan. A very familiar blue minivan.

His pulse started to pound as he eased the truck off the side of the road, nose to nose with Kara's van. She climbed from the driver's seat the same time he did, but unlike the first time they met, she didn't have a cell phone in hand. She looked as beautiful now as she had then, but a softness in the loose waves in her hair, in the simple floral-print dress, in the welcoming curve of her smile added even more to her beauty.

Almost afraid to ask what that smile meant, Sam glanced over at her vehicle. "What happened to the van?"

"What happened to the Corvette?"

"Nothing," he answered in surprise. "I sold it to my friend, Billy."

"But that car was supposed to be the first step in your plan to start dealing in classic cars. You could have sold it for so much more at an auction."

"I don't want to be going to car shows every few weeks. I want to be here with Timmy—and with you. You mean more to me than any car—" Sam cut himself off with a curse. "That didn't come out the way I meant it to."

But Kara only smiled. "Maybe to another woman that wouldn't sound like much of a compliment. But I know how much you love cars…" Her voice trailed away, but Sam read the hope in her expression.

Now or never, he thought as he sucked in a deep breath. No letting go or taking the easy way out. He was going to hold on tight and hope he survived the fall. "I love you, Kara. I think I fell in love with you right in this spot. When your father called and told me about the promotion, all I could think was that I was going to lose you and I didn't know what I would do if you left." As the words poured out, a feeling of relief swept over him and Sam realized he'd been wrong. Telling Kara how he felt was the easiest thing he'd ever done.

Especially when he saw that same emotion reflected in her eyes. "I love you. All the titles and promotions in the world can't compare to knowing you love me, too. I'm not going anywhere."

Pulling her into his arms, standing in the very spot where they met, Sam kissed her. It was what he should have done that very first day, but he vowed to make up for it by kissing her every day from that moment on. His pulse was pounding and he was struggling for breath by the time he broke the kiss. "It's a good thing you're not leaving," he murmured against her lips, "because I just remembered something."

"What's that?"

"You still owe me dinner."

Epilogue

Nothing could make a woman's heart skip a beat like the sight of a guy in a tux, Kara decided. Even if the guy was only four years old. Gazing across the dance floor crowded with friends and family, she couldn't stop smiling as she watched Timmy sneak a finger full of frosting off a piece of wedding cake. His tie was crooked, his shirt was untucked, his hair was a messy halo around his head, and Kara knew her sister was smiling down on all of them.

Thank you, Marti.

His sister's letter had been a gift, giving Kara a life and love she'd never imagined. Giving her a son and a husband and a wonderful extended family. Vince and Vanessa were slow dancing together, gazing into each other's eyes as if it was their wedding day. Nick was also dancing, but he had to split his time between the two women in his life as he took turns spinning first his wife and then his daughter around the floor. Jake was waiting hand and foot on Sophia who only had a few more weeks until her due date—a Christmas present they would always remember. And Drew was outside, helping Kara plan a surprise for Sam later in the evening.

The Hillcrest Hotel would be beautiful any time of year, but seeing the elegant ballroom with its carved mahogany trim and floor-to-ceiling windows decorated with green garland, fresh pine wreaths and red bows took her breath away. A glorious Christmas tree draped with white twinkling lights was the centerpiece of the room while miniature versions sparkled on every table.

In keeping with the holiday theme, Kara's attendants—Olivia, Sophia and Darcy—wore off-the-shoulder, deep-green gowns. All three women looked stunning even though Sophia jokingly complained she looked like she'd swallowed a Christmas turkey.

At least the dresses aren't red velvet, she'd added. *I wouldn't want all the kids to mistake me for Santa Claus.*

Despite her worries, Kara's parents had also attended the wedding. Her mother had looked incredibly elegant in a rich ruby-colored skirt and jacket and her father had looked as distinguished as always in his tuxedo. They may not have approved of her decision, but they had been there for her when she asked, and if Kara wasn't mistaken, she'd seen tears in both of their eyes when Marcus announced that he and Kathryn were giving away their daughter to be Sam's bride.

"Ready to start our honeymoon?"

Kara shivered as Sam wrapped his arms around her waist, his voice full of promise against her ear. "Ready to start the rest of our lives," she replied as she glanced back over her shoulder.

His green eyes glinted in the romantic glow of the chandeliers. “That’s my girl. Has our whole future planned out already.”

“Not all of it. Just the part where I love you every day for the rest of my life.”

“Now that is a plan I can get behind, but I hope you don’t mind a few surprises along the way.”

“Are you kidding? I love surprises.” Seeing the doubt in her husband’s eyes, Kara added, “Come with me. I have one waiting for you outside.”

Slipping away from the reception that was still going strong, Kara led the way as they stepped out into the cold, crisp night. Anticipation danced along her nerves as she waited for Sam to spot the sleek black car shining beneath the parking-lot lights. A dozen cans were tied to the bumper and the words “Just Married” were scrolled across the back window.

She knew the instant Sam saw the Corvette. He stopped short, his breath escaping in a white cloud as he stared at the car. “Is this the surprise? Billy loaned you the ’Vette?”

Reaching into her beaded purse, Kara pulled out the keys and placed them in Sam’s hand. “Billy *sold* me the ’Vette. I know you said you didn’t mind putting your plans on hold, but I don’t want you to give up your dream because of us.”

“Kara.” Sam looked down at the keys and shook his head. “I love you. It’s because of you that all my dreams have already come true. You and Timmy are all I need.”

Wrapping her arms around his shoulders, Kara leaned up and kissed him. “I love you, too, Sam. And if you don’t want to sell the Corvette at an auction, then you can consider it a wedding present.”

“So, you don’t mind keeping it?”

“Of course not.”

“See? I told you,” he said with a wide grin.

"Told me what?"

"Girls dig cool cars."

"You're right," she agreed, her lips curving up in a smile as she slipped the keys from his hand. "Which is why, from now on, you'll be driving the minivan."

* * * * *

COMING NEXT MONTH
from Harlequin® Special Edition®
AVAILABLE MARCH 19, 2013

#2251 HER HIGHNESS AND THE BODYGUARD
The Bravo Royales
Christine Rimmer
Princess Rhiannon Bravo-Calabretti has loved only one man in her life—orphan turned soldier Captain Marcus Desmarais—but he walked away knowing that she deserved more than a commoner. Years later, fate stranded them together overnight in a freak spring blizzard...and gave them an unexpected gift!

#2252 TEN YEARS LATER...
Matchmaking Mamas
Marie Ferrarella
Living in Tokyo, teaching English, Sebastian Hunter flees home to his suddenly sick mother's side just in time to attend his high school reunion. Brianna MacKenzie, his first love, looks even better than she had a decade ago...but can he win her over for the second and final time?

#2253 MARRY ME, MENDOZA
The Fortunes of Texas: Southern Invasion
Judy Duarte
Because of a stipulation in her employment contract, Nicole Castleton needs to marry before she can become the CEO of Castleton Boots. Her plan to reunite with ex-high school sweetheart Miguel Mendoza was strictly business—until their hearts got in the way!

#2254 A BABY IN THE BARGAIN
The Camdens of Colorado
Victoria Pade
After what her great-grandfather did to his family, bitter Gideon Thatcher refuses to hear a word of January Camden's apology...or get close to the beautiful brunette. Plus, she's desperate to have a baby, and Gideon does *not* see children in his future. But after spending time together, they may find they share more than just common ground....

#2255 THE DOCTOR AND MR. RIGHT
Rx for Love
Cindy Kirk
Dr. Michelle Kerns has a "no kids" rule when it comes to dating men...until she meets her hunky neighbor who has a child—a thirteen-year-old girl to be exact! Her mind says no, but maybe this one rule *is* meant to be broken!

#2256 THE TEXAN'S FUTURE BRIDE
Byrds of a Feather
Sheri WhiteFeather
Suffering from amnesia, J.D. wandered aimlessly through Buckshot Hills until Jenna Byrd offered the injured cowboy a place to stay. Slowly memories flood back to him, but what he remembers makes him want to run away from love—*fast.* Yet why can't he keep himself out of beautiful Jenna's embrace?

SPECIAL EXCERPT FROM HARLEQUIN® SPECIAL EDITION®

She thought she was free of Marcus forever—until he turned up as her unexpected bodyguard at her sister's wedding!

Read on for a sneak peek at the next installment of Christine Rimmer's bestselling miniseries THE BRAVO ROYALES....

***

How could this have happened?

Rhiannon Bravo-Calabretti, Princess of Montedoro, could not believe it. Honestly. What were the odds?

One in ten, maybe? One in twenty? She supposed that it could have been just the luck of the draw. After all, her country was a small one and there were only so many rigorously trained bodyguards to be assigned to the members of the princely family.

However, when you added in the fact that Marcus Desmarais wanted nothing to do with her ever again, reasonable odds became pretty much no-way-no-how. Because he would have said no.

So why hadn't he?

A moment later she realized she knew why: because if he refused the assignment, his superiors might ask questions. Suspicion and curiosity could be roused, and he wouldn't have wanted that.

Stop.

Enough. Done. She was simply not going to think about it—about *him*—anymore.

She needed to focus on the spare beauty of this beautiful wedding in the small town of Elk Creek, Montana. Her sister was getting married. Everyone was seated in the little church.

Still, *he* would be standing. In back somewhere by the doors, silent and unobtrusive. Just like the other security people. Her shoulders ached from the tension, from the certainty he was watching her, those eerily level, oh-so-serious, almost-green eyes staring twin holes in the back of her head.

It doesn't matter. Forget about it, about him.

It didn't matter why he'd been assigned to her. He was there to protect her, period. And it was for only this one day and the evening. Tomorrow she would fly home again. And be free of him. Forever.

She could bear anything for a single day. It had been a shock, that was all. And now she was past it.

She would simply ignore him. How hard could that be?

***

Don't miss HER HIGHNESS AND THE BODYGUARD, coming in April 2013 in Harlequin® Special Edition®.

And look for Alice's story, HOW TO MARRY A PRINCESS, only from Harlequin® Special Edition®, in November 2013.

HSEEXP0313